THE TATTOOED RATS

A NOVEL

JERRY B. JENKINS
& JOHN PERRODIN

RENEGADE SPIRIT SERIES

INTEGRITY®
PUBLISHERS
family

The Tattooed Rats

Copyright © 2006 by Jerry B. Jenkins.

Published by Integrity Publishers, a division of Integrity Media, Inc., 660 Bakers Bridge Ave., Suite 200, Franklin, TN 37067
www.integritypublishers.com

HELPING PEOPLE WORLDWIDE EXPERIENCE *the* MANIFEST PRESENCE *of* GOD.

This is a work of fiction. Any resemblance to actual persons, living or dead, is purely coincidental.

Cover Design: Brand Navigation, DeAnna Pierce, www.brandnavigation.com
Interior Design: Inside Out Design & Typesetting

Library of Congress Cataloging-in-Publication Data

ISBN 10: 1-59145-396-8
ISBN 13: 978-1-59145-396-3

Printed in the United States of America
06 07 08 09 10 LBM 9 8 7 6 5 4 3 2 1

To Jace, Jenna, Carol, Quentin, Cosette, Tad, and, of course, Patch
—John Perrodin

To Cameron, Mitchel, and Jackson Anderson
—Jerry B. Jenkins

Acknowledgments

I wish to express deepest gratitude to Jerry for giving me the chance to fulfill a dream; to David Freeman for encouraging me in freshman English; to my parents, Tom and Helen, for their support; and to my loving wife, Sue, for always believing in me.

—JP

FALL 2012

Christianity, and indeed all religion, has been declared intolerant, hate filled, and the root of all war. Thus the new world government, which calls itself the World Peace Alliance, decrees that every Christian must deny his or her allegiance to Christ or face penalties that may include imprisonment and death.

Some true believes lead double lives, pretending to be one thing while believing another. Others find hiding places—empty husks of old stores or hotels or underground caves—where they can worship God without facing mortal danger.

Trust dies as well. Friends and family become betrayers. Huge rewards are offered to those who will turn in Christians for "reeducation."

Enter the future and discover what it would be like to be the only Christian in your school.

The Kids

Patrick "Patch" Johnson:	A teen who makes a terrible mistake. How can he stand firm for Jesus when everyone else thinks he's crazy?
Amber:	Patch's friend, who wants to find freedom from fear.
Erin:	She hopes to cure Patch of the "disease" called Christianity.
Molly:	A shy, overweight girl afraid to speak out until she meets Patch.
Granger:	A basketball player who sometimes wonders if there's more to life than food, fun, and girls.
Marty:	The class bully and loudmouth. Not afraid of anyone or anything—except Claudia.
Claudia:	Known as "The Claw." She controls others by using secrets as weapons.
Trevor:	A new student, a teen with deep discernment and the ability to see past people's masks.
Nancy:	The do-gooder and volunteer at New Peace Clinic. All she cares about is making good grades and fitting in.
Gary:	A rough guy sporting a vivid collection of tattoos; the leader of the Tattooed Rats.
Tiffany:	With her bubbly personality and good looks, she's more cheerleader than Christian.
Cindy:	A sad girl who wants people to like her and who is willing to fit in at any cost.

Stan: Handsome and always able to quote the right Bible verse, he heads the most popular group of believers.

The Adults

Grandma June: An elderly woman who shares her faith through acts of kindness.

Grant Lieber: Patch's uncle, devastated by grief over the death of his son.

Cheryl McCry: Devoted to the destruction of Christians and a powerful force in the World Peace Alliance one-world regulatory system.

Linda Strong: The teacher who seeks a reward by being the first to turn Patch in to the WPA.

Dr. Max: A creative physician looking for new ways to prevent the spread of Christianity.

Ben Wattington: An art teacher and friend to Ms. Strong.

1

PATRICK JOHNSON SQUIRMED AND SAT UP, SWEATING. He scratched his scalp. Serious bed head.

What had awakened him? There it was again. The *smack-smack* of gunfire. Dazed, he scanned the store for Mom, Dad, Jenny. Oh, yeah. They were at church below. He should go to them, try to help. But he could barely move. His mother had allowed him to stay curled in his thin sleeping bag during the service. He promised her he'd read his Bible, but he'd been too sore to sit up.

Patch, tall at fifteen, was hurting. Doctors had told him he had an ulcer of the duodenum (a word he had trouble saying). It felt like acid burning away the lining of his small intestine. Worrying about the problem only made it worse. He knew he should pray more. Trust God . . . Right. So far that hadn't worked too well.

Avoiding stress would help. Bullets probably weren't good.

He wondered if anyone else was listening. People were running now, shouting. He heard the fear in their voices. He should do something, find his family.

Quickly gobbling a cracker lessened the stabbing inside, but Patch still felt sick. He hoped he wouldn't throw up like last time. Pulling himself stiffly to a sales counter, he stood, moaning.

Dizziness swept over him.

For six weeks, several families had shared floor space in the emptied-out store, Gotcha Gear. The storage room lay several feet behind him. Patch stumbled toward the door. More shots. Screams, then silence. He was afraid for his parents, for Jenny.

Should he try to find his family? Or save himself? If he could make it to the door, he could get to the hallways behind the empty storefronts at the ParkWay Mall. Escape.

He heard a child's cry. Jenny? He yanked a sweatshirt over his head, pulled on his jeans, grabbed an old pair of Nike soccer shoes and a windbreaker. Then he popped a few hard mints into his cheek. Breakfast.

Time to get outta here. Nothing he could do to help, not against guns.

No room for the bulky Bible. He stuffed his minidigicam into a deep pocket of his jacket, snapped on his watch, and took his tube of ChapStick.

Mom.

Dad.

Jenny.

The steady clomp of boots echoed in the walkways. *Get out now.* He kept low and leaped for the door handle, leaving his family behind.

AMBER WAS WARY as soon as the smiling man came to the door. What business would her parents have with this guy? Yellow teeth made his grin grimy. He wore a dark officer's uniform with a badge that read:

Inquiries & Investigations
Part of the World Peace Alliance

Always watching out for us, she thought.

"Mom! Dad! Some guy here for you." This could be exciting.

"Thanks, Amber," her dad called. "Be right down." Amber watched her father, Gerald Lane, pale when he came down the stairs and saw the stranger stepping inside. The officer ignored his outstretched hand. Her father lowered it, trembling.

"Can I help you?" he said. Amber had never seen her dad like this. Usually he joked. Now he looked scared.

"Time to leave, sir," the man said. "Come immediately and there won't be any more trouble."

Amber saw her mom pause at the top of the stairs, then turn silently and head down the hall. Amber didn't get it until the officer pointed up.

"Tell your wife to get her coat and purse."

"She's out," her father said.

Amber couldn't believe it. Her father had lied? "No she's not," she told the officer.

"Be quiet, Amber," her father said.

The man shook his head. "Come here." Amber took a step, then hesitated. The officer closed the distance, reached behind her, then yanked her wrist up between the shoulder blades. He looked meaningfully at her father. "Think you can find Mrs. Lane?"

Amber tried to pull away.

"Leave her alone," her father said. "I'll get my wife." The man relaxed his grip.

"Crystal?" her father called.

Her mom came slowly down the stairs, glaring at Amber.

"This man wants to talk with us." Her parents shared a quick look.

"What about Amber?" her mother said.

"The girl stays for now," the officer said. "Someone will place her later."

Crystal Lane reached for her daughter, held her, weeping. What was happening?

"Find Grandma," her mother whispered.

Amber was confused. "Find who?"

The officer shoved her mom toward the door. "The van's waiting."

"Mom. Dad. What's going on? What have you done?"

They looked at her. "It'll be okay," her dad said.

I doubt that.

Another officer met Mrs. Lane at the door and escorted her to the van. The WPA officer pulled an eighteen-inch silver rod from a sheath at his hip and smacked Mr. Lane's shoulder. Sparks spit and he fell. Amber stooped to take his hand, but the man kicked her away. She stood in shock and watched as they threw her unconscious father into the van, shut the door, and drove away.

What had her mom meant? Grandma was dead.

BRANDON LEIBER dug first-person shooter video games, pulling the trigger and wiping out the enemy. But he'd never imagined the pain of a bullet spray to his own chest. Now his breath leaked out as he faltered on all fours, woozy.

He fought the blackness. His dad, Grant, leaned over, his short gray hair matted with sweat.

"You okay, Dad?" Brandon slurred. His arms gave out and he collapsed.

"Quiet, Brandon." His dad held his hands, then drew him into his arms. "Gonna be okay." He patted Brandon's back. "God help us . . . please . . ." He slumped, holding his son.

HURRY. KEEP MOVING," Katy LaCaze said.

Beth walked along the sidewalk, scuffing. No questions, no talking. Her mom had warned her that someday she'd have to run.

She was prepared. Sort of. She had a small backpack with an MP3 player, a comb, and some soap. She wished she had more tunes.

Becoming a believer in Jesus hadn't been easy. Turning everything over to Christ was even tougher. Beth had thought being a Christian would be better than this. Hiding, running, praying for one more day. That was all there was to life. If not for Mom, Beth would have turned herself in long ago.

She'd seen the commercials for loyalty rewards. They flashed on street screens, in stores. It would be simple. She would be given a new family, food, time for music—and dance, her one love—if she'd only stop running. But that meant she'd never see her mother again. She'd have to turn her in. There were no rewards for silence. Mere compliance wasn't enough.

But whenever she saw her mom, Beth balked.

It helped that Uncle Wade sent text blocks of Scripture. She picked them up on her phone. Dangerous communication. If anyone found out, she could be imprisoned. Forsake your faith and live. Don't and die. Simple as that.

"Living for Jesus is exciting," Uncle Wade always said.

More like terrifying. Beth longed for the bliss of boredom.

GRANDMA JUNE! Who else could Amber's mom have meant? A back-fence neighbor, June treated Amber like her own granddaughter, giving her presents on holidays and baking her stuff for no reason at all. They weren't related, just connected at the heart.

"I'm always here if you want to talk," Grandma June often said.

Guess it's time to take you up on that.

2

Six months later

PATCH STARED AT THE ONLY PRINTED PICTURE HE HAD OF HIS family, a small wallet photo crinkled at the edges, depicting his dark-haired father, blonde mom, and smiling little sister with a peach-colored bow. All smiles.

He tried to recall their voices, but after that night, his memory was fuzzy.

Mom, Dad, Jenny, and Patch. The perfect family . . . minus three.

His cousin Brandon had also died in the church raid at the ParkWay Mall. Uncle Grant, Brandon's dad, was all the family Patch had left now, and sometimes he wished his uncle hadn't survived.

That was mean but true. To say they didn't get along was like saying cats didn't enjoy the ocean. If Uncle Grant would stop trying to replace Dad, they'd be fine.

"How can anyone be so slow?" his uncle said to Patch.

"I'm tryin', Uncle Grant."

"Try harder."

The old guy never gave him a break. Patch nodded. It was clear Uncle Grant had more to say, but Patch needed time to think. Okay, so he couldn't understand how it felt to lose your kid. But Patch knew how it felt to lose his parents and sister.

"Why did it have to be Brandon?" Grant said to himself.

Not again, thought Patch. He looked down. "You wish it had been me, don't you? It wasn't our fault. I was sick. You got shot trying to rescue Brandon and were left for dead. That's why you're here."

Uncle Grant shook his head. "No, I'm here because God wanted me here."

Thanks for bringing me here, Grandma June."

"I miss them, too, Amber," the old woman said, embracing her.

"At least now I understand what my parents believed," Amber said. "Just wish they'd told me themselves."

"I'm glad I've got a friend down in this damp cave."

"You've got several. Me, Patch, Beth, and her mom." Amber smiled. "And with your personality, young lady, you'll make many more," Grandma June laughed.

3

PATCH STARED AT TOWERING, GOLD-LEAFED TREES. Clouds fringed the bright sky. A doe stood ready to quench her thirst.

It was the same cheap poster he'd looked at every morning for months. It made him homesick for the world outside the hole he called home.

Patch felt for the deer in the picture. Pathetic. Never got to taste the water. She must be thirsty.

A throat cleared. Uncle Grant again. He had missed a button at his waist and his shirt was untucked. The man's fuzzy eyebrows arched. Patch thought of Amber's steady pleas to give her uncle a break. "He's lost a lot," she always said. Maybe she was right.

"You're a sneak." Uncle Grant got in Patch's face, pointing. "And I warned you . . ." He held the crinkled silver wrapping of a protein bar.

"I was hungry." Patch said.

"A schedule is a schedule. You had no right to eat before dinner."

"It's my bar, my ration. I should be able to eat it when I want. I don't want another ulcer attack."

Uncle Grant paced. "Excuses. No wonder things turned out as they did."

"Please don't . . ." Patch said. *No more guilt, please.* One more word and he would be sick again.

The flashing red bulbs saved him. Throughout every passageway, around each door, along the top and bottom of the walls, the glowing bloomed then faded.

The signal meant to gather for the latest report.

Pronto.

Patch dashed to the nearest widescreen monitor in his unit. Uncle Grant followed, grumbling to himself.

Another? So soon? Patch scanned the crowd for Amber. She was moving slowly, helping someone, nearing Beth and her mom. Seeing them made it seem less dangerous. More like a school assembly than what it really was.

Amber held Grandma June's arm as they hurried along. Beth and her mom, Katy, stared at the screen. Amber smiled at Patch.

The photo of a man filled the screen. He had wild black hair but was clean shaven. Handsome, a military man, a hero of the underground, working undercover at the WPA. Wade Barlow, forty-two, was Katy LaCaze's younger brother, Beth's favorite uncle.

"No!" Beth screamed. "No!" Her mother put an arm around her. Beth sobbed, heaving. "He's dead," she said. "They killed him. I know it." Though nearly fifteen, her long, straight hair and tear-streaked face made her look like a seventh-grader.

Not again." A man near Patch slammed a fist into his open hand.

Patch stood silent, waiting to see if they were right.

A female newscaster intoned that World Peace Alliance Commander Barlow was "Today's Murdered Christian." At first she pretended to care, but then she flipped her hair to one side as if doing a hair commercial.

"Officer Barlow was a man's man, a fighter, but he made one mistake," the newslady said. "One that cost him his life. He dared defy the World Peace Alliance, our beloved world government."

A stranger poked Patch in the ribs. "We've got to do something. While we can." Patch only shrugged.

THAT NIGHT AFTER DINNER, Grandma June smiled. "You're asking why, Amber?" The two, separated by nearly six decades, sat knee to knee. "If I knew that, I wouldn't have made so many mistakes. Probably wouldn't be here now. Maybe my husband's death would make some sense."

Amber crossed her arms, shivered at a cool draft. "But I never saw my parents again."

The old woman smiled. "Thankfully, they sent you my way so I could tell you the truth, help you understand . . ."

"Why didn't they tell me themselves?" Amber wasn't accusing, only sad.

"They should have," Grandma June said. "Probably would have. They were afraid for you to know the truth. And they wanted you to be old enough to see the risks for yourself."

Amber hung her head. "But the chance to tell me about Jesus— they missed that." She took Grandma June's hand. "They kept the most important secret in the world."

Patch knew what was coming. It was time for her. She scared
him, scared them all.

Cheryl McCry took her place behind a bank of microphones, wearing
a sleek white suit, her hair a shock of silver. The popular new look, thanks
to her. Her nose wrinkled as if she had just sniffed something awful.

To the younger kids around Patch, she was known as "The Beast."
Even he had nightmares about her.

The phrase "restricted transmission" flashed around the edge of
the screen. Patch knew what that meant. New televisions came with
a censorship chip. Remove the device and you triggered a homing
transmission. And that brought the Christian-haters to your location.

McCry droned on. Grandma June clucked, "If I was younger . . ."

Patch smiled. He was glad Amber had brought the old woman when
she joined the Underground. Or maybe the woman had brought Amber.
Didn't matter now. They were all part of the family.

Patch crossed his arms and leaned back against a concrete backrest.

McCry's hair stood at attention, her eyes silver slits. "We know who
and where you are. Turn yourself in while you can." She plastered on
a false smile. "Surely there are those among you in desperate need of

medical care, clean clothes, fresh water, and food. We have it all. Why suffer?" Her hands opened wide. "I speak to you as parents. Give your children what they need. Or sit and wait for us to expose you." Her image flickered and faded.

"She can't know," Patch said. "We're safe here."

The scene snapped to a basketball tournament. Bulls versus Raptors, overtime. The words "Restricted Transmission" served only as a bright border. Some shrugged and stayed to watch.

The women began to disperse and head for their sleeping chambers. Patch waited for Amber to say her good-byes. The overhead lights flicked off, replaced by the "moon glow" setting. Tricking the eye and brain with simulated day and night helped people survive the monotony, but Patch wanted a glimpse of real starlight. He knew the moon wasn't out every night like it was here in the cave.

He held out a hand to Amber, then turned at a sudden commotion.

"Seen enough?" A young man with wild eyes and spiky hair shouted, fist in the air. "We've got to find a safer location." Others nodded. Patch and Amber stood watching, also nodding. Voices knifed the air.

"Maybe McCry can help us . . . our children . . ." someone said.

"Let's move. Now!" a man shouted. "We've got no choice."

As always, debate rocked the crowd. Patch wished he could say what he felt. But sometimes the words got tangled on the way out. The crowd surged, gathered. Other voices urged caution.

"We could be doing so much more if we were in the game," someone said. "Aboveground, where we belong."

"No!" a woman yelled, her face red hot. "My husband died finding this place. We're fine. We're safe." She pulled her two boys close. The older, nearly ten, yanked free.

"They're on to us," another woman said. "Anyone can see that. We've got to move now."

Patch knew the elders would not risk relocation until they had more proof. Rumors weren't enough. It got so you were afraid to trust anyone. He could be standing next to a traitor.

Patch glanced at his uncle, a quiet, hunched man. He'd been taught that a betrayer could be someone who knew the songs and prayers, who looked the part. He'd heard that those turning in family to the WPA got a bonus. Uncle Grant would never do that, would he?

In less than a week, Patch would turn sixteen. That meant a vote in the Believer's Council. He had things to say, if he could just get them out. He'd tried his patter on Amber: "People should be free to choose escape even if being caught means execution." She had given him a look. He wasn't sure what it meant.

He pictured himself raising his fist: "No child should be forced to live in a hole in the ground. Death beats decay."

He was daydreaming again. Although truth was he couldn't tell if it was night or day living in this hole. He should be practicing his parallel parking, not hiding underground. It wasn't fair.

Amber grabbed Patch's hands. "You doin' okay?" She pulled him away from the argument.

"How's your uncle?"

"Still resentful. Sometimes I don't understand why God let me survive."

"He had reasons." Amber sidled closer. "How 'bout you?"

"Been better." He patted his stomach.

"Wanna talk?"

"No." He smiled. "Need a few minutes alone." She let go of his hand and looked hurt. "No, I didn't mean . . ."

"That's okay. When you have some time, let me know."

Too late. Amber pushed through the crowd. Patch knew he'd blown it again.

HE HADN'T MEANT TO BRUISE HER FEELINGS. He just wanted a little time by himself. He fiddled with the digicam and clicked a button to replay his last birthday party. They'd all been together then. Still happy. He watched the thirty-second clip over and over.

Jenny sat on his lap clapping, her cheeks puffed. Mom sang like an angel. He always thought she should have recorded, been a professional. Her voice was hard to hear now but impossible to forget. Dad was behind the camera as usual, his deep voice loud in the microphone.

Patch had downloaded images into a digital album on his computer. He'd been collecting snips from all his birthdays, including the first, when he stuffed his fingers into the frosting and licked the chocolate goo. His idea had been to show a close-up of his face from one birthday to the next in quick succession. Time-lapse photography of his life. He had thought it would make a great Mother's Day present.

But before he could download this scene, word came that they'd have to run. So they'd escaped to the ParkWay Mall.

And now nothing was the same.

When the gunfire started, Patch ran, grabbing only the camera, leaving everyone he loved behind. *Coward.* Sometimes he hated his decisions, choices that never went away.

He sniffed. Jenny had such a cute face, reminded him of an elf. She was small, wiry, and strong for a two-year-old. She wore a white dress with colored balloons. And she tried to blow out the candles with him.

His face showed a phony grin, way too wide. Why? Because he hadn't wanted her helping him and had gotten mad, grumbled about it until he'd eaten a second piece of cake. It was his birthday and she was always grabbing the attention. At least that's what he said then. *How stupid is jealousy?*

And foolish, he thought. To fuss about a toddler who wanted to do what her big brother was doing. One more mistake, one more thing he wished he'd done differently. Regrets didn't help now.

"Put that down when I'm talking to you." Uncle Grant's hand crept up behind Patch. Patch gulped, turned a switch, and his family faded from the mini-screen.

"What do you need?" He stood, almost as tall already as his father had been.

"I think you should try harder to get along with me. Show some respect."

Patch expected to see a long finger begin waving at his nose. "If I had my way, I'd walk out of this place. You'd never have to see my face again."

Uncle Grant massaged his forehead. "I've made mistakes, too, Patch. Sometimes I feel like I might forget to breathe, eat, since Brandon died."

Patch felt terrible. Why couldn't he ever keep his mouth shut? "I'm sorry. I miss him too."

"You can't go, anyway." Uncle Grant was all business. "Leaving this place except during approved times could jeopardize our location." He wagged his finger again. "Might get everyone arrested . . . or worse."

Patch grunted. "Guess so."

Uncle Grant put a thin arm around Patch's shoulder. "You've got a birthday coming up. Be patient. Privileges expand with age." The man smiled, his teeth dingy. "Look at me."

Patch had to grin. "Okay. Maybe it'll be fun turning sixteen underground." *Yeah, right,* he thought.

"Wait and see. You'll get plenty of time in the sun."

Uncle Grant shuffled away, muttering. Patch stopped listening. He had other things on his mind. *Except during approved times . . .* What a simple plan. All he had to do was leave when no one was guarding the exits.

So what if he'd let Uncle Grant think he'd hang around for his birthday? He was willing to say anything, tell any lie, to escape this place.

He'd had enough.

5

Patch's target was dead ahead. He had the scent, felt the fresh breeze, could taste freedom.

An opening waited thirty feet away. This was Patch's chance.

Should he escape, he'd be fair game. The bounty on a believer was huge, enough to buy a new car. But any risk beat this boring underground life.

Most of the time the checkpoint was unmanned. However, the rules stated that no one could leave except during a brief window of time when experienced scavengers slipped out for food or supplies. To go at any other time might draw unwanted attention. The times for entry and exit were planned when the helicopters were least likely to be searching.

Patch didn't care. He would get out by himself. Leave Uncle Grant on his own. Not have to bother about him anymore.

He looked behind him, stepping quietly and carefully toward the doorway that opened to the outside. Fresh air, escape. It was all he could think about. He pushed past any idea that he was being selfish, that he was risking the safety of everyone inside if he got caught, that he might want to check with Amber first, maybe take her along.

The guardhouse stood open. No one had ever tried to leave before without permission. *Always a first time,* Patch thought. All he had to do was slip through the thick steel door and he'd be gone.

For the moment, he was alone. He could breathe real air. A few steps and he would no longer feel like a dry twig at the bottom of a woodpile. The stillness swallowed him. And that sweet night air came to his nostrils through venting in the steel door. He longed to be outside.

He'd never gotten this close before. Maybe God had given him his chance. He should go get Amber and bring her along. But she'd have too many questions. There wasn't time. She might try to talk him out of this, remind him of his responsibility to others.

Forget her.

This was his chance and his alone.

"My Uncle Wade was a great guy," Beth said. "Always sending me Bible verses with his own comments. Like someone who really read the Book. He acted like God was real."

Amber looked at the photo of the deer at the brook, a weak distraction but a welcome one.

"I still don't understand," Beth said.

"Maybe we're not supposed to," Amber said. "At least not yet."

All he wanted was outside air. He didn't care whether the sky was blue, gray, or green. Anything was better than no sky at all. Patch patted the digicam in his pocket. Soon he could take pictures again of real life, living color, not underground shadows.

He ran to the steel door. All he had to do was push and step outside. Silent alarms would flash, but it'd be too late. He'd be gone. The door would close, locking him out.

He gently pushed the crossbar. It didn't give. What was wrong? Then he remembered. He needed to punch in today's code.

No problem. He knew where to find it, scribbled on a cheap chalkboard at the guardhouse. "High security," he chuckled to himself.

DO YOU EVER THINK OF LEAVING THE CAVE?" Beth asked. The two had finished praying. Amber felt a peace, a strange sense that everything was going to come together. That in the long run she'd be okay.

Amber sniffed the stifling air. "All the time."

"Would you go if you had the chance?"

"In a flash."

PATCH HEARD VOICES as he scrambled to get the code. *Oh no.* The loud talkers walked on by. *Good.* He pulled open the door to the small guardhouse, not much more than a booth with a couple of small shelves and a stool.

There it was. Today's numbers were scrawled with white chalk. This was too simple. Because things rarely went right for him, Patch expected to see some guy on guard. But no, the trusting elders only had the post active when people were passing through during the approved hours.

Patch thought it was funny that Uncle Grant had been the one to tell him about the secret code. Kind of ironic. That locked door was the only precaution. The elders just couldn't imagine anyone disobeying them.

He'd help them stop being so trusting. He read the blackboard: "1, 3, 5, 7, 9." *That was a "duh,"* he thought.

He ran for the door, flipped open the keypad cover. He entered the combination, heard a click, and shoved hard. The door flew open and he fell into the darkness, rolling down a short embankment. He heard the pneumatic hinges sigh. The door shut behind him like a bank vault.

Patch was out of the tomb.

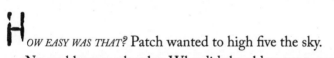

6

H*OW EASY WAS THAT?* Patch wanted to high five the sky.

No problems, no hassles. Why did the elders try to scare everyone? Not a noise out here. The night was beautiful. No danger whatsoever.

Patch saw the city at his feet. He was excited, not afraid. He smiled at the city lights, gazed at the stars. The sky was huge, larger than he remembered.

Then he saw them. *Oh no!* Shining bulks, helicopters doing their sweeps. He ducked out of sight, suddenly sweating.

Maybe the elders had been right.

Patch had to get far from the door. And fast. For Amber. For Grandma June. For Beth and her mom. Okay, even for Uncle Grant. He might never see them again, but the last thing he wanted to do was lead his pursuers to their hiding place.

A breeze gave him goose bumps. He'd forgotten even a light jacket. He'd brought just his camera and some mashed packages of crackers.

He followed the shadows that outlined the trees. The underbrush grew thicker the farther he moved down. There would be plenty of places to hide. A good half mile and he'd be safe. They'd all be safe.

But before he'd gone twenty steps a siren screeched. A voice yelled. A spotlight from a chopper exposed him. He crouched in the gravel.

"You are in restricted zone C."

Patch jumped up and tore into a run.

"Not another step or we'll shoot!"

He fell, clutching his gut. Three helicopters hovered, each aiming a glaring beam.

"Surrender for questioning," a voice boomed. "On your knees, hands behind your head."

Thwock, thwock, thwock! The vibration of the helicopters would be felt belowground. Sensors would be triggered, as well as those flashing red lights. His compatriots would gather around the big screens to watch his short dance with freedom. Patch had helped install the cameras that now eyed him.

Everyone would be watching, shocked to see him wandering aboveground during restricted-access hours. Now Patch wished he'd listened.

Too late, though. The decision was made, and he'd have to live with the consequences. Everyone would.

Some renegade. He couldn't keep out of trouble for five minutes.

7

AMBER SAW THE BLINKING LIGHTS AND WONDERED IF this was another drill. She ran for a screen. Others crouched around her, pushing to get a glimpse.

Amber saw the helicopters and a figure pinned to the ground. Something about him looked familiar. It couldn't be. He wouldn't, would he?

WHAT ARE YOU DOING OUT HERE?" a man barked loudly. He had a crew cut, and a beard crept across his jawline.

"Just camping," Patch said, forcing a smile. His stomach hurt.

"Without food, tent, or sleeping bag? Try again."

"I mean . . . hiking. Started out by those houses." Patch gestured below and started walking, "Lemme show you."

"Really?" A uniformed woman in a black cap had been listening, eyes half closed. "I'd *love* to see it."

Sweat popped out along Patch's hairline. He was hot; his stomach churned. He noticed the woman's nametag: McCry.

The Beast. Patch wanted to run. He stole a glance toward the dull silver sheen of the door. He had to lead them away.

A team of three officers stomped into the center of the 'copters. "Find anything?"

"Screen shows abnormally high readings a dozen meters back," the shortest man of the trio said, pushing up his glasses.

"Someone's down there," McCry said. She turned to Patch. "Anything you care to tell us?"

AMBER WATCHED, stunned. Beth stepped near, a shocked expression on her face. "I can't believe it."

She pointed to Patch, tiny on the screen, crouching. "He knew the WPA does its sweeps during these hours."

"They might hurt him," Amber said. *Wonder what his uncle will think.*

Amber had heard enough. Everyone was crowding in to watch like it was some gruesome reality show. She looked at the faces, pushing close like bubbles in a tub.

Where's Patch's uncle?

She dodged people, pushed against the flow and out of the room.

I'LL SHOW YOU THE TRAILHEAD." Patch stepped out of the circle. A wide hand caught his shoulder and jerked him back.

"Certainly," McCry said. She rubbed her neck. "Or should I say 'eventually'? First, we have a lead on an unauthorized gathering." She beckoned him with her long finger. "I hope you'll stay. We might need your help."

"Mom's expecting me for dinner."

"You'll have to set the table later."

McCry pushed her cap back, and spiky hair sprouted over her forehead. Patch felt the familiar sickness welling in his abdomen. The woman was white as a ghost. Her dark boots matched her black blouse. Nothing soft and squishy about her. "Innocent young men like you could get hurt if we didn't check into suspicious activities."

Patch forced himself to look into McCry's eyes, to ignore the passageway.

McCry blinked first. She scratched her cheek with a short-clipped, clear fingernail. "Maybe it's a machinery malfunction."

Patch nodded. That could be how God would get him out of this.

"Ma'am, we've found something," came the shout from an armed agent. He waved her over.

"Coming?" she said. Patch shook his head. "Fine." She jerked a thumb toward Patch and spoke to a female underling. "Keep him alive. I'll question him later. In the hospital."

8

Mr. Leiber!" Amber screamed, reaching for his knotted hands. His eyes were red. "Have you seen what's happened to Patch?"

He pushed her aside, ignoring her. "I failed him. My poor Brandon," he mused, obviously lost in some memory.

"No, not Brandon. Mr. Leiber, listen to me. I'm talking about Patch." She pulled him along. "Didn't you see the screen, sir?"

"Another drill . . ."

"It wasn't."

Mr. Leiber lifted his head, finally focusing on her. "Did you say *Patrick?*"

"We have to leave," she said as she followed him to the nearest screen.

Patch fell to his knees. *Dear God, I'm begging you. This was my fault. Save them. You've fed thousands; you could hide hundreds.*

He cringed at the cheers when officers found the opening. How could he have been so foolish?

McCry and another woman focused on the door.

"God, no . . . please," Patch whispered. *"Save them."* His guard smirked. Patch could see she wanted to join the others.

The metal panel glittered under artificial lights. A tall man yanked down dusty green strands of phony foliage. Patch had forgotten to pull them back across the door. This was all his fault. He felt like Judas.

His friends still had time. There were other exits. They could still make it. He prayed harder.

Run!"

"Hide!"

"Escape!"

Chaos, crying, screaming, pushing.

Amber held Mr. Lieber's hand. He tried to pull away. "Can we pray?" she said.

The two knelt amid the uproar.

McCry roared out a curse and pointed at Patch. She waved both arms as if directing a plane to land. The guard popped Patch to his feet.

He stumbled, caught himself, and then squared his shoulders. He would walk on his own. No way would he say one word to help. No matter what.

He walked over to McCry. She eyed him, eyes slits of reflected light. Patch smelled peppermint on her breath.

"Ready to tell the truth?"

"I ran away from home."

She eyed him. "There's more to your story."

A team of sweaty officers worked at the metal door with a mechanized crowbar. Four claws bashed and pulled at the metal panel. Patch could see it was about to cave in.

McCry held a flashlight to Patch's face. "You lived down there, didn't you?" She walked behind him. "I'm going to ask you only once. How do you open this door?"

Patch doubled over, clutching his gut. The burning was worse. "I need a doctor."

"Doctors are for the deserving." McCry turned to a woman at her elbow. "Blow a hole in the side of this hill."

PLEASE PROTECT US. Make a way out."

"And be with Patrick," Mr. Lieber said. "Protect him."

"It's going to be okay," Amber said.

She clasped the older man's neck, tears flowing. He squeezed his eyes shut. They hurried toward an exit to wait their turn, their chance to escape.

"We're trapped," a woman screamed. Her children snuffled. Caught by camera on the widescreen TVs, troops waited, raised weapons blocking their escape.

WAIT," PATCH SAID. "Please don't hurt them. I'll show you."

McCry stepped back as Patch felt his way along the metal bar. He pounded, welts rising on his fists. "Get out! Now!" he shouted toward the hidden camera.

The angry woman shook her head and a man pulled Patch from the door. He fell. "I'm sorry," he said. He knew the microphones he'd help place were picking up every word.

McCry pulled Patch to a small rise, where they stood as a blast shattered the door, exposing the ragged roofline of a cavern. Dirt and boulders slid, then settled.

G ET OUT!"

People pushed each other, confused and frightened.

Brushing dirt from her hair and eyes, Amber pulled Mr. Lieber up.

"Over there," she said, pointing. A spotlight glowed far to the left. "God's showing us the way to go."

Patch's uncle followed her, and they ran.

T HOSE NEAREST THE GAPING HOLE fled first. Patch saw Amber and Uncle Grant. She mouthed his name, but Patch couldn't move toward her. There was nothing he could do. McCry twisted his arm behind his back and smacked him under the chin, turning him to face the panicking, stampeding people.

Familiar faces caught his eye—people he'd talked with, played with, even prayed with. Uncle Grant looked at Patch. Amber tripped and fell. Patch turned away. He couldn't watch.

"Finish this," McCry ordered. Patch screamed as the second blast shattered more earth. Those still within were buried. A child's cry echoed in his head.

PATCH JOINED THE HOWL, yelling . . .

Yelling . . . His eyes were shut. He churned his sheets with his feet.

"Another dream?" Mrs. Morgan asked, her head at the door to his bedroom. Patch could hardly hear her. His hands were clamped over his ears.

"Better get up, sleepyhead."

The warden had spoken. After six weeks in custody at the Morgans' house, he knew better than to argue. *A muddy hole would be better than this,* he thought. Oh well. Another day, another chance to make a fool of himself.

HE SAT UP IN BED, STRETCHED. HIS HEAD ACHED. ANOTHER twisting, turning attempt at sleep. Another horrible vision of that night. Nothing could squeeze out the screams, the pictures in his mind. When would these images go away?

Mrs. Morgan knocked again and opened the door before Patch could answer. "Hurry up, Pat. You're not special. We all have bad dreams."

He wasn't Pat. Never had been.

"This is different, ma'am. It happened."

"When we took you in, I was told you were having nightmares. Or maybe pretending to for attention."

"It's real," Patch said.

"That's what we all think. But actually your mind is playing tricks on you. A guilty conscience, you know." Her serious face turned into a happy one. "New memories will erase the old. Now come down to breakfast."

"Yes, Mrs. Morgan." He wanted to be polite. He willed his eyes to meet hers. Then, giving up, he pulled a pillow over his face.

"Now." Mrs. Morgan chirped, slamming the door.

"A 'please' would be nice," Patch said. He yanked on his jeans and T-shirt. GOD IS DEAD! it said in blood-red block letters. He looked at himself in the mirror. Maybe so.

Patch couldn't believe he'd been at the Morgans' for a month and a half. This was far worse than living underground. He felt like an inmate already. Every day he thought about Amber, Beth, Grandma June, even Uncle Grant. They were all gone.

And it was his fault. Because he'd broken the rules, disobeyed, people had died. He deserved the nightmares.

He pulled out an old letter from his dad. "I love you, Patch. Always have, always will. God loves you too." Patch had kept it hidden. Reading it helped him survive.

Mrs. Morgan appeared behind him. She had slipped into the room again, more silent than a whisper.

"Give it to me."

She snatched the letter, scanned it, and stormed from the room.

ERIN MORGAN, SEVENTEEN, was a year older than Patch. To her he was the houseguest who wouldn't leave. "Good morning, Patrick," she said. Her hair, brown with blonde streaks, matched her mother's, though her smile was more believable.

"Whatever you say."

The two sat at the table. Placemats, matching cloth napkins, and spotless silverware were properly placed. Mrs. Morgan bustled in with a steaming platter, an egg dish full of soy cheese and organic vegetables. She served it at least three times a week. Patch was hungry. Cold cereal would have been fine. His ulcer attacks had lessened with more and better food.

He bowed his head as the others around the table shook theirs. When he opened his eyes, he said, "It *was* my fault." Mrs. Morgan stared at him. Erin sighed and the youngest Morgan, two-year-old Terrence, wiggled in his high chair.

Mr. Morgan arrived, adjusting his tie. "I won't have that tone in this house." To his smiling wife he said, "Kiss. Kiss." The stocky man sat and stole glances at the headlines in the paper. Terrence smiled beside Patch. *At least the little guy likes me.*

"I appreciate your taking me in," Patch said, "but these nightmares won't stop."

"Accepting the truth would be a good first step," Mr. Morgan said. "Maybe it would help to blame your so-called God," Erin said. "From what you say, none of this would have happened if only he had come to the rescue." Her smile was gone. She buttered wheat toast.

"Better yet," Mrs. Morgan said in her happy voice, "maybe it would help to realize that only an infinitely cruel being would allow those people to die in the first place." She turned to her husband and giggled. "Of course, we all know they killed themselves."

"They didn't," Patch said, jumping to his feet. "I've told you already, the WPA murdered them. All of them. Amber, Beth, Grandma June, my uncle—everyone."

"Stop!" Mr. Morgan's voice sounded like a slap. Terrence turned toward him, eyes curious. The father covered the child's ears. "You're confusing our little boy." He wiped his son's mouth. "Our culture is based on peace, respect, tolerance. You people have your own set of rules, beliefs, so-called moral standards. You couldn't possibly understand." Patch was ready to bolt. "What you saw was terrible. A mass suicide. It's no wonder you have nightmares."

"What I saw was—"

"A terrible mistake," Mrs. Morgan interrupted. "Not your fault, not anyone's fault. And it's time you got over it. That reminds me." She took his letter from her apron pocket. "This hardly helps." She handed it to her husband.

He read the short letter and handed it back. Mrs. Morgan stepped to the fireplace and threw the crinkled paper to the flames. "Move on, young man," she said. "It's the only way you'll get better."

"Somehow that doesn't help much," Patch said, fighting tears. "But thanks anyway. Gotta catch the bus."

"Good-bye," chirped a chorus of hopelessly happy voices.

11

"How long does he have to stay?" Erin said. "His attitude stinks." A crack of thunder signaled a spring storm.

"Coming from the expert in 'tude," her father said, "that means something."

"This is our chance to help a confused, frightened boy," Mrs. Morgan said. Erin wished she cared as much as her mother did.

"I've heard that speech before," Erin said, and her father shot her a look. "He'll be sent to juvenile reorientation at New Peace Clinic if we can't erase his crazy beliefs. I understand." Erin shook her head, pulled her long hair back, and let it fall. "I feel sorry for him, but I don't like him."

Terrence seemed to be taking in every word. "Patchy funny boy," he said.

"We've committed to keep him for a year, "Mr. Morgan said. "You were in on the family vote, Erin."

"I don't think he's good for Terry. He's scary."

The child looked surprised. "I like Patchy," he said and smashed a Cheerio.

"As good global citizens it's our duty—" Mrs. Morgan began again.

"I know, I know," Erin said. "We show him that ultimate potential is found within and that he doesn't need a 'higher being.' Blah, blah, blah. Besides, God is dead, right?"

"God is dead," Terry parroted. Everyone gave him a smile.

Patch usually sat nearest the driver, but with the rain the bus was packed. And he'd forgotten his umbrella. He was soaking. So he stood in the aisle wondering what to do.

"You know *Patrick* means 'jerk' in Christianese," Marty said, kicking him as he boarded behind him. "Stupid Christian. Don't you know rain's wet?"

"Morning, Marty," Patch said.

Marty had ketchup-red hair and rolls around his waist. He pushed to the back of the bus. Granger, a thin-limbed basketball player, swung his long legs aside. "Take a load off, Marty."

"Thanks, man."

"Can't believe that guy even talks to me," Marty said.

"Shouldn't even be allowed to ride the bus," Granger said.

Patch tried to ignore them as he scanned the aisle. He hoped for a kind pair of eyes. A hint of a smile. Anything.

Finally a dark-haired girl named Molly skooched over. She was pudgy but pretty and clutched a stack of books. Patch sat, careful to keep space between them. It wasn't easy.

"Thanks," he said. She smiled shyly but said nothing.

At school Patch dragged himself from room to room, like he'd been dumped into a foreign land and didn't speak the language. Things couldn't get much worse. Time for world history. A great way to end a bad day.

"The death of religion meant the end of war," Ms. Strong said. She was short, thin as a vine, in her forties with her hair dyed silver like her role model McCry. She pointed at Patch. "Generations ago, Christians such as Patrick murdered anyone who disagreed with their rituals. They had their own language, rules about right and wrong, secret signs, and excluded anyone who challenged them. They were, in a word, intolerant."

Patch willed himself to remain calm. He knew what she wanted. Slowly he stood. He plucked at the itchy shirt the Morgans forced him to wear, having turned it inside out in the bathroom before his first class. "Every word you've heard about Christianity is a lie," he said. Molly, goggle eyed, stared at him, her mouth agape.

Marty, Granger, and a couple of friends made hissing sounds. "Whatever," someone grunted.

"Christianity is about Jesus, not about rules or secret codes." The class lost interest. The rumbling began. "Listen for a minute," Patch said. "Please."

"Bring back the lions," Marty said. Christians used to send enemies to the coliseum to be torn apart by wild beasts. At least, that's what Ms. Strong had said yesterday. "Bring back the lions." Others picked up the chant and it got louder. Marty pumped his arm to the growing beat.

"Bring back the lions!"

Patch looked at the twisted mouths, the mean eyes. His legs felt wobbly, but he refused to topple. The teacher leaned against the video screen, arms crossed, wearing her usual smile.

Finally she held up a hand. "Dignity, class. Let's show some dignity. And compassion . . . and patience. Our goal is to help turn Patrick from his childhood brainwashing so he can see real peace."

Patch clutched his stomach and fell, writhing.

"Not again," Molly said. She popped from her seat and patted Patch's hand. He groaned and curled into a tighter ball.

"Stand back, Molly. We'll take care of him." Ms. Strong yanked Patch to his feet. She forced him out of the class into the hallway, then pushed a buzzer on her desk. The hall monitors could handle anything.

HE SAW HER FEET FIRST. Sneakers with neon-pink laces.

Patch was hunched over in a chair in the principal's office. "Hey, Erin. Nice shoes." He looked up, grinning.

She apparently wasn't in the mood. Her face flushed and she glanced around as if to see who could see her. "I've had it. I'm going to ask my parents to send you away."

"Hi, Erin," Claudia said. "*Another* garbage pickup?"

Erin moved to Claudia's desk. "Would you do me a favor? Can you keep this quiet?"

"You know me," Claudia said, smiling.

"Y OU DON'T HAVE TO SHOUT," Patch said as they walked to the car. Erin took extra-long steps and Patch rushed to keep up. The lecture went on and on as they got in the car and sped from the school.

Down the road, Erin squashed the brakes and jerked the wheel to the entrance of Gladstone Memorial Park. Tall cypress trees stood guard. She drove down winding roadways still slick from the rain.

"What are you doing, Erin?" Maybe he should get out and walk. He didn't like this.

Bouncing along the rutted dirt road, Patch held onto a swaying leather handle. Erin stopped near a concrete bench.

"Out," she said.

"What's happening?" Patch said. "Take me to your parents. I'll be out of your life for good. That's what you want, isn't it?"

"S O," MARTY SAID, "WHERE'D THEY GO?"

"That's confidential," Claudia said. She winked at him. Nothing beat being in the know.

"That's what you said last time."

"I meant it then," she said. "And I mean it now." Claudia pretended to review notes at her desk, not looking up even when she spoke. "They headed down Grand Avenue, not toward the Morgans' house."

"That means they've got another destination in mind . . ."

"Exactly," Claudia said.

Frst, I want to hear your side," Erin said.

Patch turned away grunting, "Yeah." Another setup?

Erin said, "I don't get you, don't even like you. But there's something I want to understand. How can someone as smart as you believe such garbage?"

Patch rolled his eyes. *Not again.*

"C'mon," she said. "An invisible God? Miracles. Jesus. It's all a big fairy tale, isn't it?"

Something sparked in her eyes. Hope? Did she *want* it to be true?

"Okay," Patch said. "Here are my conditions: I have my say without interruption."

Erin looked peeved. "Anything else?"

"When I'm done you can ask me anything you want, turn me over to the authorities, whatever."

Marty and Granger drove slowly through Gladstone Memorial, spotted Patch and Erin. They were sitting close. "What's that about?" Granger said.

"Something's up. Just like Claudia thought."

IF I HANDED YOU A GIFT, WHAT WOULD YOU DO?"

The sun forced its way through the trees as Patch and Erin huddled on a cold concrete bench.

"All wrapped with a bow and everything," Patch said. "Would you be curious what was inside?"

"If it was from you, I'd be scared."

"Hilarious. Okay, what if it came from someone you trusted?"

"You mean someone who knew what I wanted?" Erin smiled. "I like presents."

"So do I. And that's how the gift of Jesus was explained to me. Except he was wrapped in flesh, not paper. And he came as a baby."

"That makes no sense."

"If it made sense, no one would bother to listen. Unless something out of the ordinary happens, we ignore it. Like, look at all those ads pushing the benefits of betrayal."

"You mean loyalty rewards."

"Call them what you want," Patch said. "You see people on exotic trips, riding in convertibles, dancing, smiling, and hugging. The images attract your attention even though you know it's not possible. Nothing will ever make you as happy as the people you see in the ads."

"So . . ."

"So if some old man showed up in a robe one day and said he was God, you'd think he was crazy."

Erin started to say something, but Patch held a finger to his lips. "No interruptions, remember? The story of Jesus' being God's Son, of his coming to save the world, is either too fantastic to be true or too incredible to be made up. One or the other."

Erin shook her head.

"Look, people don't die and then come back to life, do they?" he said, wishing he could see into her mind.

"No," she said.

"Jesus did. He died for us and was raised from the dead."

"That's just a story."

"Exactly. It's a story, a report, a tall tale. Or . . . is it true?"

MARTY SCRATCHED HIS HEAD as he sat in his car watching. "Wonder what they're talking about."

Granger wondered too. "Never thought that freak would be Erin's type," he said. The two passed a small pair of auto-zoom binoculars back and forth.

"Me neither."

"Maybe we should do something about it," Granger said.

"Or at least get close enough to hear."

LOVE," PATCH SAID. "That's why."

Erin was about to respond.

Granger, crouched in the bushes, pounded Marty on the shoulder. "What?" he whispered. "You hear that?"

"Smooch-time already?" Marty said aloud, standing with a grin.

"We were just talking!" Erin said, looking like she was about to cry.

"We thought maybe you were in trouble," Marty said. "Being alone with the weirdo."

"We're fine," Patch said. "She's safe. You can go." He tried to stand but Granger held him down, hand on his shoulder.

"Leave him alone," Erin said.

"I thought we were friends, 'Rin."

"Don't call me that."

"Well, what could you see in this skinny Christ-Kid? He's nothing but trouble."

"Agreed," Erin said. "That's what I was trying to tell him."

Words failed Patch.

"So you're ready to leave?" Marty asked.

"And how. He's been trying to convince me Christians aren't the enemy."

Patch felt that familiar tremor in his gut and took a deep breath. *Two-faced* didn't begin to describe her. "I need to get going," he said.

"Another tummyache?" Marty said. "Poor thing."

"Faker," Granger said.

Erin took Patch's arm, but he yanked himself away and headed for her car. He glowered out the window at Marty and Granger slapping a high five as Erin got in without a word and started the car.

GRANGER WATCHED THEM GO. With his long legs, he looked like he walked on stilts. That's what made him a great basketball player. "Was he trying to ask her out?" He shrugged, confused.

"Claudia was on the mark again," Marty said, adding another clod of gum to his wad. "Good thing she had us follow them." He blew a pasty-blue bubble and grinned at his friend.

Granger leaned on the back of the red car, Marty's sixteenth birthday present. "What was with the 'love' talk? Erin couldn't be interested in that freak."

"Girls don't think like we do," Marty said. "Maybe he really was trying to sell her on the whole religion thing."

"Or she's lying."

They jumped in the car and Marty backed out of the park.

"Watch that tree!" Granger hollered.

"You sound like my mom."

"And you drive like my grandpa."

SO HE FELL MOANING AGAIN," Molly said. "Right in class."

Her father looked up from the flat-screen TV. "Indigestion?"

"Daddy, you're not listening." Molly turned to her mother, cropping photos on her laptop.

"Of course we are," her mother said, kicking her husband's ankle. He revived and blanked out the television with his mega-remote.

"You're worried he might be contagious?" Molly's dad said.

"Never mind." Molly headed for the kitchen, but her mother stopped her.

"So why do kids treat him that way?" Her mother looked concerned.

"He is a *Christian*," her father said. "He has no more rights than any common criminal."

"The Morgans shouldn't have taken him in," her mother said. "Nothing but trouble."

"I'll call the principal," Molly's father said. "I won't have my little girl frightened in class."

Molly caught a glimpse of herself in the reflection of the dark TV. She hadn't been Daddy's little girl for some time. "No, that's not what I'm asking." It was so frustrating.

"Don't worry, sweetie," her mom said. "That boy won't be bothering you anymore."

Mom. It happened again." Marty was shoveling in Doritos, his favorite snack.

His parents hadn't lived together since he was a baby. Marty had no memories of his father. No pictures, no visits. Nothing.

"This stupid kid, some religious weirdo the Morgans are trying to retrain . . . He's always disrupting class and trying to tell people that they have to believe in Jesus and stuff."

"You're kidding. I had no idea that kind of thing was allowed in school." His mother stood and paced. "They sure shouldn't."

"Yeah . . . I just don't want to get confused, is all."

"Enough is enough. In this day and age, there should be no more danger of young minds being poisoned by ancient lies."

"Gonna grab a Coke, Mom," Marty said.

"And I'm going to make a phone call about this. First, I've got a few things to research."

Marty's plan had worked. His mom was on a mission, and Marty knew he wouldn't see her again that night.

What was that about, Erin? I thought we were having a real discussion."

"I was trying to get rid of them," she said. "I didn't know what else to say."

"So you made me look like a fool."

"I'm sorry, okay?" They pulled into the driveway. "But I want to talk more."

More games.

"Forget it," he said.

"Please, Patch."

So she was serious? Maybe she deserved another chance.

"Lemme think about it." He walked to the house like he was heading for a final exam he hadn't studied for.

Principal O'Connor knew a trend when he saw one. Three contacts from parents in one morning was enough to scare any administrator. He didn't want word to get back to the World Peace Alliance Education Office.

"Well, I'm sorry. We certainly don't want our children exposed to dangerous thoughts, especially in school." Mr. and Mrs. Jacobs, Molly's parents, were easily soothed. Mrs. Stephens, Marty's mom, was more difficult.

"You have no right to allow my son to hear treason, filth, and lies. That kind of thinking was outlawed years ago."

"You're absolutely right," Principal O'Connor said. "And it won't happen again."

"Better not," Mrs. Stephens said, slowing. "If it does, I'll sue."

14

Little Terrence Morgan chased the doggie around the room. It flipped, growled, and played tug-of-war with a plastic rope. Terry held the other end. He pulled, but the puppy held its ground. Erin tapped the intensity button on the robotic canine, easing it down to give Terry an advantage.

With a yank the boy flipped the metal bundle of gears and wires into the air. It rolled and landed on its feet like a cat. "*Bark! Bark!*" it emitted, ready for more.

Erin watched Patch head upstairs to his room. She turned to follow, but her mother said, "Got a minute?"

Erin stopped.

"I got a call today from Principal O'Connor."

Erin sucked in a breath, then forced herself to relax. "Is the school trying to raise money? Please don't make me sell candles again."

"No," Mrs. Morgan said, her expression serious. "Did you have more trouble with Patch today?"

Erin shrugged. "He got sick, so I drove him home."

"Well, I think there's more to that story."

"Didja do it?"

"Sure, Marty. I told my dad what you said. 'Bout how I was hearing religious stuff in class. He blew up."

"So did my mom."

"O'Connor must be getting worried," Granger said.

"He better be. Or else we'll sue." The two laughed.

Patch listened from the top of the stairs.

"He can't go back?"

"No, Erin. He's been expelled."

"That's not fair."

"I thought you'd be happy, sweetie. Aren't you the one who wants him out of the house?"

"Yeah, but how will he learn anything if he's not in school?"

"They have programs for boys like Patrick. Special medicine to help him think in new ways."

"Mind control?"

"He'll be okay." Mrs. Morgan patted her daughter's arm.

"Just getting what he deserves," Erin said.

Stop crying, Molly. Have a couple of cookies."

"I'm not hungry," she said, sniffling into a Kleenex.

"Just made them." Mrs. Jacobs sniffed. "They'll make you feel better."

Molly grabbed two large ones. The chocolate chips were melty.

"You did the right thing in telling us."

"But I didn't mean to get him in trouble."

15

I UNDERSTAND, SIR. I'LL MAKE IT CLEAR in class tomorrow." Ms. Strong put down her cell phone. Principal O'Connor's orders were clear. She would tell the class Patrick had been hospitalized for ulcers and wouldn't be able to attend school anymore.

She wrote: *No more Patrick.*

PATCH DIDN'T HAVE MUCH TIME. They would be coming soon. He threw clothes into a duffle bag and pulled candy bars from his bottom drawer.

He heard a knock.

"Who's there?" He spoke quietly.

"Me. Erin."

He didn't want to see her.

He zipped up his bag of balled-up clothes and opened the door. "I'm leaving. Don't have to worry about me influencing Terry anymore."

"I'm sorry."

"For what?"

"For acting like you were crazy," Erin said.

"That makes me feel better." He rammed a drawer shut.

"You can't go back to school," Erin said.

"I heard you and your mom. Glad you think I'm getting what I deserve."

They were interrupted from downstairs. "Erin!" her mom called. "Phone!"

"Don't do anything till I get back, Patch. There's something I gotta tell you."

Patch moved to the window and saw the van coming, lights flashing, no siren.

WHEN ERIN PICKED UP, Molly Jacobs introduced herself and said, "I'm in Patch's history class."

"He can't come to the phone."

"I want to talk with him," Molly said. "But I don't think he'd want to talk to me. I'm the one who got him in trouble."

"What? How?"

"I was telling my parents about class, and they thought I was upset. But I wasn't. I was just curious. They never understand."

"Hang up, Erin," Mrs. Morgan said. "They're here for Patrick."

"Molly, I've got to go."

"Just tell him 'Sorry' for me. Please."

The front door opened, and two men in dark-blue uniforms entered.

Mrs. Morgan pointed upstairs.

When they brought him down, the taller man carried Patch's bag. Terry looked up from playing. "Patchy. Look, Patchy."

"Patrick has to go away," Mrs. Morgan said. She eyed Erin. "It's for the best. You'll see."

16

Ms. Strong tapped a plastic ruler on the edge of her desk, and the jabbering faded with Marty's whinny of a laugh. "You may have noticed," she began, "that we have an empty seat today."

Marty started the cheer, and Granger joined in. The roars picked up. Only Molly paid attention.

"Patrick will no longer be with us."

"Is he dead?" a boy said. Marty guffawed.

"No." Ms. Strong smiled. "But he isn't well. He has both physical and mental problems. You saw that firsthand yesterday. Can anyone tell me what was wrong with him?"

From the front row came Nancy's quick reply: "He believed a lie." It wasn't a question. Ms. Strong could always count on her.

"Exactly. He believes God literally exists. That Jesus is the son of God and the Savior of the world. Fairy tales . . . Yes, Molly."

"I thought maybe . . . ah, maybe he's not here because he disagreed with you."

"What?" Ms. Strong felt as though she'd been slapped.

"Maybe he knows what he's talking about, I mean. What if he's right?"

Marty booed. "Or maybe he's your boyfriend."

"Molly Jacobs, come here." The girl squeezed out of her chair. "Go see Principal O'Connor. Immediately." Ms. Strong pushed a button at her desk, and the WPA monitors marched to the door.

"So you heard?" Claudia asked, blue eyes shining.

"I was there," Marty said. "Molly is so pathetic."

"What do you mean?" Nancy said, joining the others at the table. The three gobbled sloppy joes plopped onto plastic trays.

"You don't get it, do you?" Claudia smiled. "Molly has nothing going for her so she's willing to try anything to belong. Believe whatever someone tells her."

"Loser," Marty said.

"She always seemed sweet to me," Nancy said.

"She's weak minded," Marty said. "'Easily led,' my mom would say."

"I don't know . . ." Nancy's voice trailed off.

"Watch yourself, Nancy," Claudia said, pointing a finger. "Or we might have to talk to Mr. O about you."

Patch sat in a dark room. Prison-issue bunk, thin sheet, flat, smelly pillow. Toilet in the corner. "Oh God," he prayed, "what now?"

The door swung open and a white-clad team of three pushed a wheeled box in, bottles and pills piled high. Long needles gleamed.

"What's that?"

"Silence!"

"Relax, Dr. Max," a tall woman said. She wore an enameled button that declared: *Veggies have rights too!* It was emblazoned with a carrot wearing a scarf around its slotted "neck" with one gloved fist raised high. "The boy can ask anything he wants." She smirked. "Of course, we don't have to answer."

The other member of the trio, a woman with curly black hair, looked down. She was an orderly, the least of the least in the ward. Orderlies knew it was usually best to keep silent, especially when the bosses laughed. Patch noticed that an animal, a roaring lion, was tattooed below the short sleeve of her scrubs.

"What is all this?" Patch asked, looking at the gleaming silver tray of medications.

"Don't worry," Button Lady said. "We're professionals." She held out a hand. The silent orderly handed over a syringe, cringing. Button Lady tapped the needle as clear liquid spurted from the tip. She plunged it into Patch's thigh. The orderly gasped.

More laughter as Patch jerked from the pain.

17

Pincipal O'Connor could have been St. Nick's bald brother. Of course, Molly didn't consider herself anything to look at either.

"I'm told you disrupted the class." Mr. O scratched his bare scalp.

"I thought we were supposed to ask questions when we didn't understand things." Molly blew her nose into a soggy Kleenex and squished it in her thick hand.

"Throw that thing away." He pushed a trash can toward her. Everyone seemed to love telling her what to do. "We've never had any trouble from you before."

"Curiosity is trouble?" Molly said.

"Your parents are coming," he said, rising and moving toward the door. "You just sit and think until they get here."

Ms. Strong sank into a beat-up couch in the teachers' lounge. "What a morning."

"What's wrong, Linda?" a male colleague said.

"Something strange happened in class."

"You're a teacher, remember?" He smiled. "That's normal."

"But one of my kids stood up to me," she said.

"C'mon! That's common."

"But not for this kid," Ms. Strong said. "She's a wimp."

THE ORDERLY HAD SEEN IT MANY TIMES but still felt sympathy for the patient. Dr. Max pulled open Patch's eyelid. "Drugs taking effect. Pupil response is slowing." He let the boy's head sag to the side. The tattooed orderly stepped closer, eased Patch to his cot. She did the grunt work, the heavy lifting.

"We'll watch him, Doctor," Button Lady said.

The man tapped his foot. "Take careful notes. And remember slow speech and the inability to control his muscles will be typical."

Button Lady poked the orderly in the ribs. "Acts like he's teaching us something."

The orderly shut her eyes, sighed. *Poor kid*, she thought.

WE'RE ASHAMED OF YOU," her mom began.

"Ashamed?" Molly said. "What did I do wrong?"

Her parents looked stunned.

"You're not listening," Molly's dad said.

"Yes, I am. I'm politely asking what I did wrong." Molly was frustrated but determined. "Can't I have my own ideas and opinions?"

"We didn't think you had any," Mrs. Jacobs said.

18

PATCH GASPED, AS IF WAKING UP UNDER WATER. Moving his fingertips took all his concentration. His body refused to obey his mind.

Where am I? The room looked familiar. Drab, cold.

Who am I?

TWO WEEKS POST-PATCH HAD FLOWN BY. Nancy never heard his name anymore. She sure didn't miss him. When Ms. Strong announced the after-school volunteer program at a local facility, Nancy raised her hand. A new opportunity to serve.

"Nancy Nightingale to the rescue," Marty said.

"What's wrong with doing something worthwhile?"

"I've got better things to do." The redhead clawed at his scalp.

Granger high-fived Marty.

"Nancy's right, of course," Ms. Strong said.

"Of course," Marty mimicked. "She always is."

"Would you like a trip to the office, young man?" Marty slumped in his chair. "No more negativity," she said. "We must all do our part."

MOLLY LISTENED TO THE BANTER, sat up straight. It was time.

She raised her hand, and the class quieted, stared.

"Um . . . You never really answered my question from before."

Marty's grump turned to a grin.

"What question was that?" Ms. Strong said.

"My mistake," Molly said. "Actually it was two questions. First, was Patch kicked out because he disagreed with you, and second, how do you know he was wrong?"

Ms. Strong seemed to struggle for control. Molly crossed her fleshy arms and waited.

ERIN PICKED AT HER SPAGHETTI. Nice, normal family meal.

"Where's Patchy Boy?" Terrence said.

"I told you," his mom said. "He decided to live somewhere else."

"He decided?" Erin said.

Her father gave her a *Drop it* look.

"Where is he?" Erin had to know.

"He's a sick boy," her mom said. "He's in the hospital for a few weeks."

"Can we visit?" the little boy asked. "That'll make him better."

"No visitors," Mr. Morgan said.

"Puppy misses him," Terry said.

Me too, Erin thought.

MR. O EXPELLED MOLLY, and nothing could have made her happier. She wouldn't miss class, kids, or Ms. Strong. Her punishment was to work at home, alone, which was better than being pointed at. She would keep up with her assignments online, watching classes via video monitor. But she was forbidden to comment.

Fine. She would write instead.

Molly's Manifesto, she scrawled. *I vow not to say one more word until I get an answer to my two simple questions. As a student, I have a right to be treated with respect and allowed to think for myself.*

That was only the beginning. This could be fun. Maybe she could get extra credit in English class for journaling.

NANCY DRESSED CAREFULLY THAT MORNING, choosing pale pink pants and a white top. No buttons, bows, or anything fancy. She wanted to look the part of a nurse's assistant's assistant on her first day at the New Peace Clinic. Her sensible shoes squeaked, new and white.

A male administrator handed Nancy a printout listing the patients she would sit with, talk to. She could hardly wait. This would be great.

"I'll see the same people every week?" He nodded.

Many of the patients were asleep or glued to their TVs. They ignored Nancy's chatter, waved her away. She went from room to room. In one, someone sat staring out the window. Only it wasn't really a window. It was a light panel with a wooden frame for examining X-rays. "How are you today?" Nancy stepped closer.

"Hello," the tired voice said. She could barely hear him.

"I'm Nancy. What's your name?" John Jones, her list said.

"I don't know." He turned, his face pasty, eyes dull.

Patch.

19

LONG PLASTIC TABLES STOOD IN ROWS UNDER BRIGHT SKYLIGHTS. Trees had been painted along the walls, and overhead loomed some generic puffy clouds. A picnic without the ants.

Claudia sat across from Erin. Granger came in from the left and Marty from the right. She was trapped, like it or not.

"Whatever infected Patch got Molly too," Marty said.

"Something weird's goin' on," Claudia said. "I never thought Molly would make a peep in class. Now she's expelled."

"I heard," Erin said. "Don't have to worry about us, though. I'm sure we'll never see Patch again."

Claudia gave Erin a weird *So what?* look. She held her hand up, fingers curled. Her famous "claw" sign and source of her nickname.

And he's probably forgotten all about me, Erin thought.

MOLLY WORE GRAY SWEATPANTS, too big even for her. Who cared? They were comfortable, and no one saw her. She liked not worrying about what to wear. She poured a double serving of cereal and doused it with milk.

"Morning, Molly," her mom said.

Molly smiled thinly and nodded.

"I said 'Good morning!'" Her mother came closer, expecting a response.

Molly carried her bowl to the table, held up a finger, and hustled from the kitchen. She returned with a long scroll, curled tightly, tied with a satin ribbon. She handed it to her mother and sat to eat.

Mrs. Jacobs pulled the ribbon. "Molly's Manifesto."

Her mother read on, jaw sagging. Then she called for her father. "Honey, c'mon here. Quick. We have a problem."

NANCY WAS SHOCKED. How could someone look so different in only two weeks? And Patch didn't even act like he knew who he was. Maybe it was the medications they were giving him.

"Patch? Is that you?" Nancy crept closer. It couldn't be. He looked tired, a shadow of the boy she remembered from class.

"Jones" turned toward her, face blank. "Who are you?" It was barely a question, his voice was so weak. Nancy sat and took his cold hands.

"Don't you remember me? I'm Nancy, from school." She shivered.

"I'm sorry. I don't know you." He stared at the panel of lights, his forehead lined. "What did you call me?" he said, looking back at her.

"Patch."

"Like what covers a hole in your jeans?" He shook his head and giggled a strange, nervous sound. His eyes returned to the glowing white lights. "Pretty," he said, pointing.

Nancy nodded. "How are you doing today, John? John Jones."

"Thought my name was 'Patch.' You're weird."

"My mistake," Nancy said.

HER FATHER'S VOICE BOOMED. "The silent treatment? What kind of stunt is that?"

"What are we going to do with you?" Molly's mother said.

Molly hurried to her room and yanked her laptop off her desk. Her parents followed. Molly typed: "What did you say, Mom?"

"I said, 'What are we going to do with you?'"

"Simple. Answer my questions. Please?"

THIS WAS IMPOSSIBLE. Nancy leaned close. "Don't you remember me? We sat in class together." Nancy put a hand on Patch's shoulder. "What have they done to you?"

Patch stared, obviously confused. "Who are you?" he said.

"Stop it!" Dr. Max stomped into the room.

"Sorry, sir," Nancy said, cheeks flushed. She stood and faced Dr. Max. "I was only trying to help."

The doctor grabbed Nancy's wrist and led her out the door. "That boy is very sick. Questions will only upset him."

"He looked lonely." She squirmed from the doctor's grip. "I thought I was supposed to befriend the patients."

Dr. Max gently tucked Nancy's arm into the crook of his own. He strolled and she stepped quickly alongside. Staff zipped past posters that reminded everyone to wash hands. "I appreciate your compassion, your concern. But you must let the professionals take care of the boy. Or he'll never get better."

"What's wrong with him, Doctor?"

"Brain damage. Car accident. Only survivor."

THE FEMALE ORDERLY CHECKED THE HALLWAY before slipping into the clinic barber shop. The man with the razor gave her a quick wink. Patch's hair fell to the floor like overgrown grass. He sat, eyes glazed, expression sad.

The woman whispered. "You think it's him? Sure fits the description."

"Could be." The barber's biceps bulged. "Hard to believe one scrawny kid could cause so much trouble. We've got to help him." Snakes writhed, dragons flexed as his tattoos moved. They looked at the tired teen. "Keep an eye on him."

The orderly agreed, patted the big man on the shoulder. Then she was gone.

20

LINDA STRONG'S HANDS SAT ON HER HIPS, silver-white hair plastered to her head. No lipstick. "Things will change here," she said. "Our guest will explain."

"Good day, students," Principal O'Connor said. Muttering greeted him.

"Ms. Strong tells me that you've been giving her trouble." He paced like a tiger. "That will end now."

Marty gave a low, *Oh–I'm–so–scared–of–the–principal* whistle.

"Was that you, Martin?" Mr. O said. Someone giggled. "Did I say something funny?" Silence.

Nancy curbed the urge to raise a hand.

"Patrick was a troublemaker. He's gone. Molly asked disrespectful questions and has also been banned. Do you want to be next? I will have peace in this classroom at any cost." Principal O'Connor scanned the room. "That's better. Let's just get along."

CLAUDIA LEANED CLOSE TO NANCY at lunch. "How's your new job going? Seen any cute patients?" Nancy felt Claudia pumping her for gossip.

"Depends on your taste. Patch is there. And he didn't even recognize me."

"He was pretending. Trying to get sympathy," Claudia said.

"He doesn't even know his own name."

"What's he doing there anyway?" Nancy kept silent. A car accident, brain damage, Dr. Max had claimed. Nancy decided to keep that detail to herself.

MOLLY WONDERED IF MR. O REMEMBERED that she was watching via live video feed. He looked funny on TV. The camera, mounted high in the back of the room, caught his glistening baldness.

She wished she could join the class discussion, ask some questions. Mr. O's short speech wasn't much of a show, not very entertaining. But Molly's voice transmission had been muted. She couldn't have commented even if she wanted to.

After class she e-mailed a note to Nancy.

Mr. O was real scary, huh?

AFTER SHE HAD TIME TO THINK, Nancy decided that Patch's problems could be the key to open the door of popularity. After all, it was the first time "The Claw" had shown any interest in her. Might be fun to be cool for a change.

"C'mon. He didn't know who he was?" Claudia asked. "You're kidding."

"Nope." Nancy enjoyed the attention. "He's lost his memory. Or it's been stolen from him."

"Guess it's for the best," Claudia said. "The old Patch didn't fit in. Maybe the new one will."

"You think he'll come back here?" Nancy asked.

"Of course. Then Mr. O and Ms. Strong can talk about how they've successfully"—Claudia lapsed into a robot tone—"trained a young mind to follow the path to truth and wisdom."

"Stop," Nancy said. "You're weirdin' me out."

"Kind of like Patch?" Claudia smiled.

"Actually, yeah."

THE NEXT DAY NANCY'S E-MAIL RESPONSE came back to Molly full of sincere-sounding nothings. So she *could* e-mail classmates. Good.

"Molly's Manifesto," now pushing two pages and growing, contained thoughts about truth and whether or not it was knowable. It was ready to send to the entire school.

Of course, the e-mail system wasn't for personal use. That required special permission.

Molly hit Send anyway.

She stared at the monitor and saw kids nudging each other. Some turned to the camera and gave a thumbs-up. Soon the whole class was studying their screens.

Ms. Strong leaned over a computer, then tore from the room.

Tell Mr. O I said hi, Molly typed, and tapped Send once more.

YOU BELIEVE THAT MESSAGE FROM MOLLY?" Nancy sat with her new friends.

"Not sure what's she's talking about," Claudia said, "but she's braver than me."

"What should we do about the other thing?" Nancy said.

"What other thing?" Granger said.

Nancy told him about Patch.

"That I've got to see," Claudia said. "Bet Marty would want in. Listen, next time you visit the hospital, give me a call and take Zombie Boy for a ride in a wheelchair to the far north fence. If anyone can make him remember who he is, Marty can."

"I'm not sure that's such a good idea," Granger cautioned.

Nancy thought about that. It might work. It couldn't hurt.

"But you guys have got to be nice to him," she said, gathering her backpack. She felt torn, hoping to fit in, but also wanting to help Patch.

"You know us," Granger said.

21

CALM DOWN, LINDA. IT'S NOT YOUR FAULT." They sat in the teachers' lounge, about the size of a storage shed.

"But she was my student." Ms. Strong took the coffee from colleague Ben Wattington. "I should have handled the whole thing differently."

"You couldn't know. And don't take this wrong, but Molly's quite a good writer."

Ms. Strong gave him a look. "You're kidding, right?"

"I was surprised at her e-mail. Clear. Intelligent. Her questions make sense. I've wondered some of those same things since I was a kid." A pair of teachers stopped talking.

Linda leaned toward Ben. "I'd keep my voice down if I were you."

WHAT A NICE IDEA. A surprise party," Marty said. "Complete with ice cream and toppings."

Granger never knew when Marty was joking. "Thought you two didn't like the guy."

"I hate him and everything he stands for."

"So what's with the treats?"

"They're not to eat."

MOLLY WAS AMAZED HOW EASY IT WAS. And she couldn't believe the e-mails she got in return.

If there was a hell, you'd be going . . .

You're crazy.

And those were the nicer notes. Some threatened Molly's life and family. Even her cat.

But many of the kids cheered her. "Way to go" and "You're the woman!" were here favorites. She wondered how long it would take for this to reach her parents. Until then, she'd keep writing.

"GOOD ONE," LINDA STRONG SAID, forcing a laugh. "You're funny, Ben."

"What?" His brow furrowed, his glasses sliding lower on his nose.

"People are listening," she whispered with a pasted-on smile. "You want to be reported?"

"What are you afraid of, Linda? Mere ideas?"

Ms. Strong snatched up her coffee and left.

Ben shook his head, feeling the eyes of the eavesdroppers.

MOLLY DIDN'T HAVE TO WAIT LONG. Sharp raps at her door. "Molly, may we come in?"

She still wasn't talking, so she just opened the door. Her parents stood with arms crossed, a wall of irritation. Molly shrugged and held her hands open, palms up, as if to say, "What's up?"

"You know why we're here," Mr. Jacobs said.

Molly raised her brows.

"Honey," her mom said, "we think you need to see a doctor. To make sure everything's okay."

Molly flopped onto her bed and reached for her laptop. She typed, "I'm fine. Just looking for a few answers."

"We know. But we think a professional might be able to help."

Molly snapped the computer shut. She was misunderstood whether she wrote or spoke. So she wouldn't do either.

"Come in," her father said, and two stocky young men in dark blue entered. Marched right in.

MR. BEN WATTINGTON CHASED MS. STRONG like an elementary kid chases a friend. "Hold up, Linda! Please!"

Ben lengthened his stride and caught her by the elbow.

"Get your hands off me," she said.

"I thought we were friends," he said.

"I'm going to Principal O'Connor."

"About what?"

"What do you think? Your subversion."

SHE'D GOTTEN PERMISSION without a raised eyebrow—enthusiastic, immediate approval to take Patch for a stroll. So Nancy and he took off, she pushing his wheelchair. The New Peace Clinic grounds sprawled, the summer grass thick. But should she go through with this? She hadn't asked permission for him to greet old friends.

"Hey, Patch . . ." Marty called from the other side of the fence. Claudia and Granger watched his face. A large cooler sat on the ground near them.

"Patch?" Patch said, blankly.

"You must remember," Claudia said, flashing her best smile. She opened the cardboard lid. Ice cream, and plenty of it. "Hungry?"

"Is there enough for me?" Nancy said.

"Absolutely," Marty said, standing on tiptoes and reaching over the fence. "Hold out your hands."

"Not funny," Nancy said. "Didn't you bring cones or cups?"

He shook his head. "Guess we'll have to eat out of the box." Marty reached the chocolate-vanilla-strawberry ice cream over to Nancy along with a couple of spoons. "Friends don't mind sharing, right?"

"Neapolitan is my favorite," she said. "Want some, Patch?"

He turned his head as if in slow motion. "Sure." She handed him a spoon and held the box for him. He dug out softening curls of cream. "Great," he said, licking the strawberry first.

Claudia, Marty, and Granger stood watching. "Aren't you guys eating?" Nancy said.

"After you," Claudia said. She leaned over and pulled from the cooler three canisters of whipped topping. Plastic caps popped off, and the three shook the cans and took aim. Billows of whipped cream flooded Nancy and Patch. Nancy wanted to run away, but she wouldn't abandon Patch. She jumped in front of him, covering her eyes. Patch sat laughing, covered.

Claudia and her cohorts dropped the cans, grabbed the cooler, and ran.

Nancy felt like crying. How would she explain this mess to the hospital staff?

"It's okay," Patch said calmly. "Maybe you can wheel me through the sprinklers. That would be fun." He acted like a child excited about a day at the park.

He seemed so harmless, so innocent. Nancy thought how strange it was that nuts like Marty, Claudia, and Granger ran free while a nice kid like Patch was stuck here. She pushed him toward the revolving sprinkler heads. "Time for your shower, sir," she said with an English accent.

23

WE DON'T HAVE TO DO THIS," Molly's father said. He took her smooth, thick hand. "Just say the word, and this foolish game will be over. Any word . . ."

Molly shook her head.

The men led her outside. Her posters, stuffed animals, and music would stay behind.

Molly refused to cry. She mentally added to her manifesto more questions for her teacher, her parents, and herself.

She was belted to a bench in a panel van, guards stationed in front and behind her. Another man sat at the wheel. The back windows had been painted over. Only the driver could see where they were going.

Molly closed her eyes.

YOU GUYS ALL RIGHT?" The dark-haired orderly hurried over, towels over her arms. Nancy offered thanks. The two were soaked to their socks. Her shoes squeaked as she stepped onto the patio to curious stares. Patch sat with his head lolling, looking exhausted.

Dr. Max met Nancy and dismissed the tattooed employee with a sniff. "What happened this time?" His cheeks puffed in and out, pulse thudding on his squat neck.

"Sprinklers came on," Patch said dully. "Wasn't her fault."

"It is a hot one," Dr. Max said.

"Exactly," Nancy said. "We were trying to cool off."

"Next time ask first," Dr. Max said.

Nancy hurried Patch to his room.

"Medicine time," a woman said, pushing a steel cart. She didn't seem to notice that Nancy and Patch were dripping. Pills filled up small plastic cups. "Mr. Jones . . ." She checked a box as she handed them over.

"Yes, ma'am," Patch said.

"I'll see that he takes them," Nancy said, taking them from him.

The woman gave Nancy a quick look. "Now, all right? He's got to take them right away."

ERIN COULDN'T BELIEVE SHE WAS DOING THIS.

She would say it was little Terry's idea, his fault they were heading to the hospital. Terry was in a car seat kicking, holding his plastic dog tight.

"Patchy Boy will want to see me . . . and puppy."

"I'm sure he will," Erin said. *If he remembers you.*

At the sign-in desk, a skinny man ran his finger down a list of names. "Sorry. No one by that name."

"You sure?"

"The list is confidential," he said. "Or I would let you look for yourself."

"So, I don't suppose I could show my brother around anyway. Since we drove so far?" She wasn't used to pleading.

"No, I don't suppose," the man said, standing.

The glass doors whizzed open as they walked out. At the entrance two men were helping an overweight girl out of a van. Her long brown hair hung in clumps. What could be wrong with the poor thing? She didn't appear ill or injured. She caught the girl's glance.

Molly. Molly Jacobs. What in the world?

That was Erin Morgan! Molly realized. *Didn't look like she even knew me. Or maybe she pretended not to.* Molly couldn't blame her. This place was for crazies. So why would Erin be here?

As Molly walked with her guards down one locked hallway after another, she felt like a rat in a maze.

THE NEXT DAY AT SCHOOL Claudia met Nancy at the door. "Aw, c'mon. Can't you take a joke?" Nancy kept walking as Claudia followed. "Didn't you guys think it was funny?"

"Patch is sick! Don't you get it? I can't believe you did that to him."

"Just trying to cheer him up. Listen, did you hear the latest?" Claudia pulled Nancy to an opening in a bank of lockers. "Molly's been taken to the New Peace Clinic. I heard Mr. O talking to her parents."

PATCH POPPED THE PILLS INTO HIS MOUTH, but the minute the orderly left he spit them into his hand, then flushed them. He kept his back to the camera's eye. Skipping the drugs was something he'd been doing ever since Nancy told him he had a choice. That was after that cold shower in the sprinkler outside. The water woke him up.

Since he'd gotten to New Peace he'd been obediently swallowing the pills, but even so his fog was beginning to clear. The medicine wasn't working like it used to. The tattooed orderly always gave him an expectant look when she handed over the medicine, as though she knew a secret. *Something strange about her,* Patch thought.

To everyone who saw him, he was still the doped-up, easygoing John Jones. But in reality he was starting to think again. Starting to remember.

And starting to fear.

PEOPLE WERE PLAYING WITH HER MIND. Molly knew it. There was constant piped-in music, a wall of TV monitors, each playing a different program. Sound was a weapon. Impossible to find even a moment's peace with medications every few hours. That must be the point. They were wearing her down.

Molly wasn't allowed a computer or even pen and paper. Her parents couldn't visit. She was alone.

But not completely. Someone seemed to be speaking to her. She felt a strange peace amid the noise. Maybe she *was* crazy. Molly had to concentrate to finish a single thought. So she blocked everything else out. She felt calmer the noisier things got. That wasn't her.

Normally she blubbered when she was stressed and gobbled snacks to hide her unhappiness. No longer. After a week, Molly was eating less and doing a lot of pacing around her room.

Can it ever be wrong to ask an honest question? Whatever happened to the idea there is no such thing as a foolish question?

Molly walked on.

THE NEW PEACE BARBER kept busy enough. Lots of hair to cut, especially with the staff stopping in for a trim now and then. On break, he stood looking at the vending machine options. The tattooed orderly sauntered over, coins in her open palm.

"Ladies first," the big man said.

The woman popped the change in. A diet drink smacked down. "What do you think?"

"Almost 100 percent sure that it's him."

"Should we talk to him?" The orderly took a sip, eyes darting.

"Don't know if he's ready. Not with all those drugs clouding his mind." The big barber looked worried.

"I've been slipping him sugar capsules for a couple of days. He should climb out of his fog soon." The woman took a final gulp, tossed the can in the trash.

24

Hmmm. Hmmm, hmmm, hmmm, hmmm.

What was that tune? So familiar. Then it came to him.

"The Bible tells me so . . ." Patch sang quietly. Things were coming back. Bits and pieces. A girl's face, an old woman, a familiar-looking man. Maybe he'd even remember who he was and what he was doing in this place. Every day his world came into sharper focus. He sensed a peace, a protection.

It felt like someone was watching out for him. At last.

Look at the two of them." Granger adjusted the volume.

"Makes me sick," Marty said.

"Never seen anyone so slick."

Marty shushed him. Granger could tell Marty was concentrating just like he was, headphones snug. They stood behind a clump of trees as far from the main building as possible, watching Nancy push Patch's wheelchair. Granger was concerned. When they were out of sight of the facility Patch jumped from the chair and ran small circles around the girl.

Granger caught Marty's eye. Through digital binoculars he watched Nancy smile. Marty fiddled with the receiver and pulled in more of their conversation.

"Nancy, it's all coming back," Patch said.

"Slow down." Nancy put her hand on Patch's shoulder and he settled. "We've got to think. Plan."

Ever since Patch had passed her in the hallway and told her quietly to "check beneath her lunch table," Molly had been afraid to look. Finally, she got the courage to peek underneath the table, while picking up a napkin she'd purposefully tossed to the ground. She didn't see it at first. Then, there it was, a piece of paper he had taped under the table for her.

Twelve slow weeks had ticked by. Isolated, she'd had nothing to do but walk, exercise. She only ate until she felt full and had never felt so good.

And now this, a secret message.

It was a sheet torn from the Holy Bible. In the margin it said: *Dear Molly, I remember you. God does too. He knows we're here and he's here for us. I'm praying for you. Patch.*

Tears welled. They'd been held back a long time.

The page was from a book called Matthew. She had never seen anything from the Bible before and didn't understand why it had a man's name on it. Wasn't it supposed to be about God? Questions flooded her mind.

Some of the words were in red and some in black. There were numbers, big and small, plus notes at the bottom of the page. What did it mean? Molly's eyes slowly dropped to a small headline that said, "The Parable of the Sower."

Patch was concerned when he saw Nancy's expression.

"I never should have found you that Bible," she said. "I was reported to the school and to my parents. I told everyone it was for an art project. I'm probably being watched." Nancy pressed her hands together.

"Sorry, but thanks," Patch said. If Nancy knew he was using pages from the Bible to send messages to Molly, she'd be even more frightened. He changed the subject to his escape plans.

"Impossible," she said after he explained.

"I know," he said. "That's why I need your help."

25

"FIRST YOU ACCUSE A CO-WORKER OF TREASON," Principal O'Connor said. "Now this."

"Nancy trusts me," Ms. Strong said. "She's afraid she might get kicked out if this goes any further. She wants to go to college."

Principal O'Connor didn't appreciate talking to a teacher's back. "Look, no one else is having these discipline problems. Maybe you're not teaching with enough energy. We all get burned out at times."

Ms. Strong turned and gave a look that was easy to interpret. "Nancy as much as admitted her involvement."

"She's a stellar student," Mr. O'Connor said. "Her parents are wealthy—they lead this community. I'm not about to accuse their daughter of being a traitor without more evidence."

"Then I'll prove it."

CLAUDIA COULDN'T WAIT TO TELL THE OTHERS. It was time to let Nancy know she wasn't part of their circle anymore. Or not. Maybe Claudia would split the reward if Nancy confessed something to them and the authorities used it to convict her.

News . . . Must talk. ASAP.

Claudia pecked out the letters with her pink stylus. She signed the note *The Claw* and hit Send.

MOLLY DIDN'T KNOW MUCH ABOUT CROPS, but she still wondered why "the sower" was so careless that some of the seeds fell by the wayside, some on stony places, and some among the thorns. Wouldn't it be more efficient to plant only in good soil? She looked at the notes at the bottom of the page.

Sometimes strong winds blew the seeds into the roadway or among weeds. Some soil was shallow with rocks just below the surface. Roots didn't have room to grow. That's why many of the seeds merely sprouted and wasted away or were eaten by birds.

What was Patch was trying to tell her? Was he accusing her of being like rocky ground? Patch hadn't written the Bible. If there was a message for her, it wasn't from him.

"He who has ears to hear, let him hear!" *What in the world does that mean? Of course I have ears; we all do.* Sure she must be missing something, Molly read from Matthew 13 over and over.

ERIN CALLED NEW PEACE CLINIC, asking to talk to patient Molly Jacobs.

"Nobody here by that name."

"Okay. Thanks." Erin hung up.

But she'd seen Molly there. What was going on?

JUST SIGN HERE," the nursing assistant said. "We'll take care of Molly."

Molly's mom looked pleadingly at her husband.

"She still refuses to talk," he said. "Nothing has changed." He put his arm around his wife. "We have to trust these people to do what's best for her."

"But she's our daughter. Shouldn't we be the ones trying to help?"

Mr. and Mrs. Jacobs stared through the one-way glass where Molly sat at a table. A pair of female physicians asked question after question. She refused to meet their eyes and finally shook her head, letting her eyelids close.

"See?" Mr. Jacobs said. "We can't give up. That would be the worst thing for her."

Mrs. Jacobs signed.

Molly RELAXED AND A LONG BREATH GUSHED OUT. Another session with the "kind and friendly" doctors was over. She'd tuned them out, let her thoughts wander. They didn't scare her as much as before, but she was glad to be in her cell, to have a break from the questions.

She waited until an orderly passed. Then she read the torn page for the umpteenth time.

"He who has ears to hear, let him hear!" Who was this Jesus? Why was he talking about seeds getting eaten by birds or falling on stones? Molly couldn't understand. Or maybe she wasn't listening.

She wanted to get it, to see why Patch was willing to stand up to an angry class for what he believed. But it didn't make sense. Nothing did.

She didn't like that most of the verses were negative. Positive thinking was all she'd been taught since she was too young to remember. But the Bible told it like it was. Nothing was held back or sugar coated. Young plants got scorched in the blistering sun, struggling sprouts were choked by thorns. Then it hit her.

She thought of the class yelling, "Bring back the lions!" She saw Patch's frightened face, his sad eyes. It was horrible.

And she knew.

He was that young plant trying to grow, to spread some shade. The other kids were the thorns, squeezing the life out of him. She was getting closer now. The words meant more than what they said on the surface. Digging out the deeper meaning would take more thought.

Great. I have nothing but time.

26

For the whole semester, Nancy spent most of her volunteer time with Patch. When she started she was hoping to find some tidbits for Claudia, but now she did it because she cared. She was in Patch's room when Dr. Max popped in.

"How's our patient today?"

"Mr. Jones is still listless and doesn't seem fully aware of his surroundings."

"Where's puppy?" Patch shouted. "Where's poochie? Doggie-dog?" He showed his teeth. Dr. Max jotted a note.

"Clearly delusional," Dr. Max said. "Thinks he's a dog."

"I thought he was asking for a puppy," Nancy said.

Max gave her a sympathetic look. "Psychology isn't simple. You must look for deeper meanings, see below the surface."

Nancy nodded.

Patch growled and barked, and Max checked the list of meds. "This kid needs higher doses." Patch slid out of his chair, then rolled to all fours and sniffed. He made a face when he got to Max's shoe.

"I'll sit with him until he's quiet," Nancy said.

"Let me know if anything else happens," Dr. Max said as he fled.

Nancy turned to Patch. "It would be easier to keep track of the times you *don't* do something strange."

"Woof," he said with a grin.

MOM, DO WE HAVE ANY EXTRA BIRTHDAY CARDS?" Erin asked. "Funny ones. The school calendar lists the birthdays of every student." She wanted to send a card in care of Molly's parents.

"Check the middle desk drawer in my office," her mother said from the kitchen.

Erin pulled open the wide drawer and was lifting papers, searching for cards, when she saw an envelope from New Peace Clinic. She knew it would be wrong to snoop. She had no business peeking. But New Peace was where Patch was being treated and where Molly was staying. Erin slipped the envelope from the drawer, curiosity overcoming guilt.

THERE SHE IS," Marty said. He, Claudia, and Granger sat waiting. Nancy was leaving New Peace Clinic. "Show time."

If their plans worked they would split a reward, enough to keep them stocked with music and movies for months. Ms. Strong said so.

"Looks happy," Claudia said. "She's got a thing for that Patch guy. A girl can tell."

"Shut up," Marty said.

"Whatsa matter? Afraid of the competition?" Claudia taunted as Marty gave her a dirty look.

Claudia's car was basic but fast enough. They followed Nancy onto the freeway.

Marty leaned hard into Granger and shoved him into the door handle. "Keep your mouth shut about Nancy."

NANCY LOOKED INTO HER REARVIEW MIRROR. Someone was following her. The windows were dark blue. A pink flower twisted around the driver's sideview mirror.

Claudia! And she probably had her goons Marty and Granger with her.

Why were they trailing her?

LOOK, SHE'S PULLING OFF!" Granger shouted.

Claudia swerved two lanes over. Horns blared, but she made it.

"Nancy's onto us," she said.

"Then get closer. What's the difference?"

BELOW THE LOGO—an arm with bulging biceps—and address for New Peace Clinic, the director of clinical placement had typed:

> *To whom it may concern:*
> *For your records you may be interested to learn that Patient X, male teen, brown hair and brown eyes, has been reclassified "John Jones." Should you need further information regarding proof of identity to claim a tax deduction, simply call this number.*

A toll-free phone number followed. Erin couldn't believe it. Patch was gone and had been replaced by John Jones. *Wonder what they call Molly now?*

"What are you reading?" Mrs. Morgan stood at the doorway.

27

Nancy pulled into the parking lot of Chicken Chunks and leapt from her car.

Claudia leaped in two spots over, and Marty and Granger emerged.

"Hey, Nance," Marty said. "How's it goin'?"

"Why are you following me?"

"We're just worried about you," Claudia said.

"Right."

"Yeah," Marty said. "We heard about your trouble with Mr. O and wanted to help."

Claudia's look appeared to shut Marty up.

"What trouble?" Nancy said.

How dare you?" Erin's mom snatched the letter. "This is private."

"Why the lies?"

"No one's lying. They're trying to help Patrick."

"Why change his name?"

"They're hoping he won't be the same person when he comes out. Less belligerent. Less of a brat."

Finally, honesty. "You never liked him?"

"Where did you get your first clue? He wasn't my idea. Your dad's the do-gooder. I agreed only because we got a double tax deduction to feed and house him. How else can the government get people to do the *right* thing?"

SHE SAID WHAT?" Nancy's cheeks flamed. She had to get out of here.

"It's true, Nancy," Claudia said. "I head them talking. Ms. Strong thinks you've become one of them, whatever they call themselves."

"The term is *Christian*."

"You'd know," Marty said.

"Anyway," Claudia said, "we figured the best way to clear your name was to see if you were still the same Nancy we all know and care about."

"So, what, you follow me so you can run me off the road and ask me?"

"You've been acting weird," Marty said, "spending too much time with that loser."

"I like my work. Hope to be a doctor someday."

"Always shooting high," Marty said.

"Nothing wrong with that," Granger said. For the first time, Nancy noticed his smile.

"Do you want hang out with us tonight?" Claudia said.

That came out of left field. Nancy didn't trust her. "I guess."

"Pizza okay?" Claudia smiled.

PATCH STARED OUT THE WINDOW, hands clasped behind him, listening. His slowness and stumbling were an act now. He perked up his ears for any detail that might help him escape.

A thin-faced maintenance man talked to a coworker. "Great. They party and we get to clean up their mess."

"It's a big deal," the other said. "A bunch of guys from the school."

"The usual dog-and-pony show. But there should be lots of leftovers, tubs of food to take home to the kids."

Patch let his lids droop and his head flop back. *Interesting possibility.*

M OLLY FOUND ANOTHER PAGE from Patch underneath the art room table. "The Parable of the Sower Explained" noted a small subheading right above verse 18 of Matthew chapter 13.

Verses 19-23 said:

> When anyone hears the word of the kingdom, and does not understand it, then the wicked one comes and snatches away what was sown in his heart. This is he who received seed by the wayside.
>
> But he who received the seed on stony places, this he who hears the word and immediately receives it with joy; yet he has no root in himself, but endures only for a while. For when tribulation or persecution arises because of the word, immediately he stumbles.
>
> Now he who received seed among the thorns is he who hears the word, and the cares of this world and the deceitfulness of riches choke the word, and he becomes unfruitful.
>
> But he who received seed on the good ground is he who hears the word and understands it, who indeed bears fruit and produces: some a hundredfold, some sixty, some thirty.

Molly closed her eyes. No way could she understand this without help. Enough with the pen pal thing. Time to talk to Patch face to face.

28

WHAT'D Ms. STRONG SAY?" Marty said when Claudia hung up.

Claudia grinned and made her trademark "claw" gesture. "If we get evidence against Nancy on video, she'll split the reward with us—half for her, half for the three of us." Granger furrowed his brow.

"Can't ask for more," Marty said.

"'Course we could," Claudia said, "but we don't want to be greedy."

PATCH READ: *Must meet. Please. Too many questions, not enough answers. M.*

Maybe he and Molly *could* meet and talk. After nearly four months, the two weren't watched much anymore. The hospital staff wouldn't expect either to say a word—Patch because they thought he couldn't, and Molly because she hadn't, and wouldn't.

Patch stripped out another page of the Bible. He hated tearing God's Word apart, but in this case it was necessary. He pulled out a pen. *Cafeteria, far corner. Behind big Chinese vase with ugly flowers. Late lunch. Quiet.* Patch drew a tiny smiley face and taped the sheet beneath the table.

ERIN POPPED THE BIRTHDAY CARD INTO THE MAILBOX. She liked sending mail the old-fashioned way.

She wanted to find out more about Patch, do something if she could. And Molly. It was clear she had been given a new identity too. How could a parent allow that? What could have been so horrible that New Peace look liked the answer for their daughter?

CLAUDIA POPPED UP from her seat and hugged Nancy like a long-lost pal. "Love your hair."

Almost like a real friend, Nancy thought, and she couldn't keep from smiling. The pizza smelled good too. For once, she didn't even mind Marty and his sidekick being there. She had begun feeling funny about how Granger acted around her.

"Tell me about your volunteer work," Claudia said.

"Seems real important to you," Granger said.

"It is, Grange." Weird, but she liked his gray eyes. "You can't believe the improvement in some of the patients."

"Like Patch?" Claudia said.

Nancy shrugged. "Sure, he's doing better. But . . ."

"But?"

"He's not Patch anymore. He's got a new name: John Jones."

"What's up with that?" Claudia asked.

"Just one of the secrets of New Peace." Nancy enjoyed confiding.

"Tell me more," Claudia said.

IT'S LIKE WE'RE SPIES," Molly whispered. Patch let his head flop, keeping up the act in case anyone was watching.

Patch's reputation cleared space at nearby tables. No one wanted to be around when he started his next animal impersonation. He hoped it would keep working to let the staff think he was nuts, though they were bound to catch on sometime.

Molly's face was thinning, her cheeks flushed from exercise. Barely edible meals probably helped too. She looked happy, Patch thought. He had never looked into her eyes before. He liked the openness he saw.

"So what's the point of the Sower story?"

"What did you get out of it?"

"I guess the seed is God's Word. It comes to each of us in some form or another."

"Right," Patch said.

"But does that mean our hearts are either rocky ground or the thorny ground? Aren't we just born the way we are? I mean, if for a moment I say God exists, wouldn't it be his fault for making my heart hard, or rocky, or full of weeds?"

Patch smiled. "Tough questions. Here's what I think: God's Word is God's Word. It existed from the start." Molly nodded. "But we change. Constantly. And that's why we have such trouble understanding God."

"He's always the same and we're always shifting" Molly said.

"Right. Constantly changing, falling, failing. That's what makes it so hard. It's like the Bible is completely clear, but we have on glasses that make it blurry."

"Is there a way to take them off," Molly asked, "or at least clean them?"

"Prayer is the answer, Molly."

"Is that all, Patch? I've prayed to my inner spirit, the sun, the moon, and once to a box of Rice Krispies bars. There's nothing to prayer."

"Prayer only works when you pray to the one who can answer."

"AND YOU'RE NOT GOING TO BELIEVE THIS," Nancy said, enjoying their hanging on her every word. When she laughed, they laughed. She was the center of it all. Granger had gotten up to get her more Coke. Twice.

Her phone rang. "Got to get this first." Nancy clicked the Talk button. "Hello? Hey, Erin, great to hear from you . . ." Claudia and Marty exchanged a look. "Sure, I could help you, but I'm in the middle of something right now. Can I call you back? Thanks!"

Nancy slapped her phone shut. "Now where was I?"

Claudia and the others chattered, all asking questions at once.

That was a weird call, Nancy thought. *Why would Erin care so much about Patch and Molly?*

She saw movement out of the corner of her eye. A flickering tongue . . . yellow eyes? . . . Someone, some*thing* was watching.

"What did Erin want?" Claudia said.

"Yeah, what's the big secret?" Marty said.

29

I CAN'T PROMISE FIRE FROM THE SKY OR INSTANT CHANGE, but prayer works on you from the inside."

"Are you saying that there's something deep-down wrong with me?" Molly's eyes bore into Patch's.

"Exactly. That's why we need a savior."

"But how do I know he'll even hear me?"

"The Bible promises that." Molly was obviously suspicious and a little afraid. "Go ahead and see for yourself." Patch made sure no one was listening to them. "You've tried everything else."

"I'll think about it."

"Good. But don't take too much time." Patch winked and walked away.

HAD THEY PUT SOMETHING IN HER COKE?

Nancy's head spun and she saw things she couldn't be seeing. A preening rubbery lizard perched between Claudia and Marty. It had green, shiny scales and a row of horns poking out over lidless eyes. A six-fingered claw sunk into Claudia's shoulder. But she seemed to not even notice.

The creature stared at Nancy, and when Granger reached to touch her hand, she jumped.

Didn't Claudia feel those piercing nails? Nancy tried to push past her, but she was trapped. Claudia sat talking and talking and talking. Faces went in and out of focus. Claudia's voice swelled into a high-pitched whine then slowed.

Nancy couldn't stand any more. "Don't you see it?" She slipped under the table to the floor in a ball.

Granger shoved Marty out of the way. Claudia leaped to her feet. "Nancy! What's wrong?" She nudged Nancy with her foot.

Granger got the manager, who brought ice in a plastic bag.

"Thanks, man. We'll take care of her."

Nancy tried to crawl from between the booths and bumped her head on the edge of the table. She grabbed her shoulder bag, groggy. Claudia took one side, Granger the other. Marty led the way.

When Marty tripped he looked back to see what had made him stumble. Nancy pointed at the thick, twitching tail. "No!"

HERE GOES," Molly said to herself. She felt weird, self-conscious.

"Um," she whispered. This sure didn't feel comfortable. It was like talking to herself. Unless of course someone was out there listening. That's where she was having problems. If Patch was right, why didn't more people believe like he did.

She realized maybe she was afraid. What if she found out this prayer thing was one more big lie?

Try it, she told herself. *What would it hurt?* Patch seemed like a guy she could trust. Alone in her room, she looked from side to side, closed her eyes, put her head down.

"Molly here. Not sure how this works, but I need help."

THE VIDEOTAPE ROLLED. "She wasn't loud enough for long enough," a mole told Dr. Max. "But we have her lip movement. Maybe amplification will help."

"Good work," Dr. Max said. He smiled. "Some sort of spiritual transmission tactic."

"Does that volunteer— What's her name?"

"Nancy," Dr. Max said.

"Does she know how close Molly and Patch are getting? She must have brought him that Bible."

"Keep watching. I need hard evidence."

SO CAN YOU DO IT?" Erin said.

Nancy tried to focus on her face. "Sure." Everyone was pulling at Nancy, picking at her, trying to get her to do things she didn't want to do.

Erin put a hand on Nancy's shoulder. "It's the only way to help Patch."

At least no beady-eyed creature perched on Erin's head. That had to have been because of something she ate. It was too impossible to be true.

FOR GOD SO LOVED THE WORLD . . ." Ms. Strong tossed the book onto her desk. "What in the world are you reading?"

"I told you," Nancy said. "It's for an art project.

"Don't you see 'Forbidden' stamped in red across the front page?"

"Of course," Nancy said. First the meeting with Erin. Now this. "I got an okay from Mr. Wattington."

Ms. Strong squinted. "You did, did you?"

"I'm creating an Ancient Myths mobile for the District Art competition. I signed the 'Education Purposes Only' release form. So did my parents. I'm cutting out the illustrations and replacing the faces with tiny mirrors. My art teacher thinks it could win for creativity."

"I had no idea."

WHEN NANCY GOT TO A WATER FOUNTAIN she had to hold on to it to keep from falling.

No one knew she had bought two Bibles. She had found them in a beat-up old box at the back of the used bookstore.

With the covers torn off, who could tell where one volume began and the other ended? Nancy gave one to Patch and kept the other in her bottom drawer under some sweaters. Something drew her to the book.

One thing was certain: no one must ever find out.

30

"Look, Doctor. Her lips keep moving, but there's no sound. Sorry the audio is so weak."

"Worthless, actually." Dr. Max's phone rang and he stepped into the hall.

"No good," he reported. "We have no hard evidence . . . Look, I tried . . . I'll keep trying."

"You can't leave me, Patch. If you're escaping, I'm going with you."

"Molly, I don't think we could both make it at the same time without getting caught."

"Why should you go first?"

"It's not that I want to leave you behind." The memory of Amber's face flashed in his mind. "Maybe there'll be room for you."

"Why do they do it?"

The Shining One shrugged. His younger charge always had questions, and this was a good one.

"They're only human." His voice flowed like a mountain waterfall, clear, ringing. "Since they were created few have learned to pray first, act second."

The young angel cocked his head. "Always get it backward, don't they?" The Shining One nodded, his wings tucked tightly at his back.

"But God will use even this. No mistake need ever be wasted."

D<small>O</small> YOU THINK IT'LL WORK?" Erin said.

"Sure." Nancy felt better. She'd gotten some sleep and stayed away from Claudia except to trade phony greetings in the hall. For some reason she missed Granger. "They won't ask questions, Erin. They're desperate for volunteers. But I feel weird about lying."

Erin took a quick peek over her shoulder. "We gotta help Patch."

Nancy had been reading small doses of Scripture as she tore out the black-and-white illustrations for her art project. The words spoke of purity, of being free from deceit and "falsity." She had never minded telling a white lie or even a whopper for a better grade, but now that didn't taste right. What was wrong with her?

"Yeah, I guess," Nancy said. "As long as we're doing it for a friend."

W<small>E</small>'RE CRASHING AND BURNING," Claudia said as kids sped past in the hall.

"Quit ranting." Granger said. Then, seeing Claudia's expression, he put up his hands, surrendering. "Thought we were trying to keep things tight. Secret."

"Grange is right," Marty said. "Things'll work, but we have to keep quiet."

"I want that money," Claudia said. "Ms. Strong will find someone else if we don't deliver."

Ms. Strong beckoned the trio. The three straggled across the hall like they were being led to a pop quiz. Ms. Strong pulled the door shut and stood with her back to their exit. "Anything? Tell me!"

"We're close," Claudia said. "Still lookin'."

Ms. Strong nearly fell over as the door opened.

"Sorry. Don't lean on the door." It was the art instructor, Mr. Wattington. "Wondered if you were free for lunch . . ." He saw the students.

"Gotta run, Ms. Strong," Marty said. Seeing their chance to escape, the three rushed out.

THE VOLUNTEER ADMINISTRATOR gave Nancy an over-wide smile. "Erin Morgan. Referred by our Nancy here." She handed her a guidebook and a laminated badge. "Clip this on. You must wear it at all times. Nancy will show you around." Erin couldn't believe the thick manual, assorted handbooks, and a dictionary full of counseling terms.

"Here," Nancy said. The two split up the books. "I'll take half. Patch is down that hall. Hurry."

THANKS A LOT, LINDA," Mr. Wattington said. "Principal O'Connor just finished chewing me out. Then I found out about your accusations against Nancy."

"Quite the busybody," Ms. Strong said.

The man smiled. "I have a confession," he said. "I let Nancy use a Bible for her project. Don't try to get her into trouble for something I approved." He paused then added, "Please."

"But you know it's a banned book," Ms. Strong said.

He shrugged. "Sometimes I like to rock the mucky-mucks upstairs. Nancy's actually tearing up the Bible for her project, using the pictures. In a way, she's desecrating it."

"So you're not an undercover believer?"

"You've gotta be kidding. Anything's okay with me in the name of art. Even recycling an old collection of fairy tales."

31

I DON'T DO WELL IN CRAMPED SPACES," Molly said.

"Maybe praying would help," Patch said.

"It'll be dark and we'll be smooshed in the back of the van, but I think we can do it."

Molly gave Patch a one-way hug.

NANCY AND ERIN swept into Patch's room together, but it was empty.

"Where would he be?" Erin said.

"No idea," Nancy said, grabbing his chart and sliding her finger down the page. "He's been given grounds privileges."

"Meaning?"

"He can walk whenever and wherever he likes. Chart says he needs more exercise."

"Let's wait and surprise him."

WHAT'S THAT WRAPPED AROUND YOUR NECK?" Granger said.

Marty wore a collarless shirt. "Um . . . skin?"

Granger backed away, looking terrified. Marty watched him take the stairs two at a time, leap to the landing, and bound down the rest.

Funny, Marty thought. He did feel a little strange. He scratched at his throat. It felt tight, itchy.

Allergies. What else?

YOU SURE IT'S OKAY?" Molly said.

"People stopped caring about us a long time ago," Patch said.

"Like my parents."

"Molly, I wasn't trying to remind you. Hurt you . . ." Patch said. They were outside his room.

She touched a finger to his lips. "Don't worry," she said. She took his hand and opened the door.

I'M HONORED, PRINCIPAL O'CONNOR. I'm sure Mr. Wattington will be able to go too."

Ms. Strong hung up her cell. The principal had called from home saying he was sick and couldn't attend the evening's gala at New Peace Clinic. His wife didn't want to go alone, so two seats had become available.

Good food, glitz, twinkling lights. She could dress up. She rang Mr. Wattington and invited him.

"You do *have* a clean shirt?"

"Nice . . ."

"That's a compliment. You immerse yourself in your work. I like that in a man." She hung up, blushing. She couldn't believe she'd said that. *I'm too old for these games.*

Nancy! Hey! And Erin!" Patch let go of Molly's hand and introduced her.

"How are you, Molly?" Erin said. "It's been awhile. You look fantastic. New hairstyle?"

"And I've lost a little weight."

"So how'd you get in?" Patch said.

"Nancy pulled some strings."

"You all should catch up," Molly said. She kissed Patch on the cheek. "See you tonight." He blushed.

So WHAT HAD GRANGER SEEN?

Marty steered toward the restroom and stood at the mirror. "You rock!" he said, pointing at his redheaded reflection with both hands. He looked closely at his neck. No marks, no blemishes. Perfect, except for that prickling sensation.

"Whatever," Marty muttered.

The creature looked into the mirror and reached clawed digits to its own skull, imitating a comb going through hair.

"Whatever," it mouthed silently.

32

PATCH NEEDED ANOTHER HAIRCUT. He knew he looked raggedy, but the clinic barber used only an electric razor and Patch always ended up looking like a prisoner. Not much choice. It was the official cut for guys at New Peace.

As the barber worked, Patch checked out the tattoos all over his arms. Horned beasts. Demonic stuff. Why would a guy do that to his body?

"You got any tats, dude?" the barber said.

"Huh?"

The hulking man pointed to his tattoos as he buzzed Patch's hair off. "Tats. Tattoos."

"No." Patch wished this monthly ritual was over.

"People don't see the heart in the ink," the man said. Patch didn't have any idea what he was talking about. He wished the guy would stop talking so he could sit and think.

"Yeah, they're great," Patch said without any conviction.

The barber began humming. He'd gotten the message.

Patch used these few stolen moments to wonder about that funny feeling he'd had when he saw Erin again. He was glad to hear Terry was okay. And he still got a charge out of her smile when Nancy told about his famous dog impression.

Then came the Molly Discussion.

Erin had started the ball rolling downhill. "She's sure changed. Looks beautiful."

Patch nodded, but he didn't want to reveal Molly's experiments with prayer or her study of the Bible. "Good to have her around. True friends are hard to come by."

"Maybe more than friends?" Nancy said. Erin looked around the room.

"That's our business," Patch said, suddenly irritated. "You know, I'm tired of being a germ under your microscope. Maybe you should leave." Erin and Nancy had looked stricken and left without another word.

Patch wished he'd pushed Erin more, asked her if she was ready to take a step toward Christ. He still wondered about that.

"All done," the tattooed man announced.

"Thanks," Patch said, feeling the short stubble on top.

"What, no tip?" the barber said.

Patch grinned as he left the chair. That guy wasn't so bad—not nearly as scary as he looked.

Ms. STRONG PULLED ON A BLACK SWEATER that hung past her shoulders like a cape. Buttoned close at her neck, it showed off her silver shirtdress and thin waist.

She decided to make the best of the evening. Ben wasn't bad once you got past his so-called humor. She looked forward to time with him. Just the two of them. Sort of. Too bad there would be kids around.

Finally, the doorbell.

"Stunning," Ben said when she opened it.

Ben wore a white shirt, bow tie, and blue blazer with his standard-issue navy khakis. Clean but just informal enough to raise eyebrows.

"Not bad yourself," she said.

33

I'M GOING," Claudia announced.

"You weren't invited," Granger said.

"They promised a free meal to anyone willing to sing in the choir for the New Peace dinner," Claudia said.

"You don't sing." Marty imitated her raspy high voice doing the musical scales. "You can hardly hum."

"I mouth the words," she said. "Have for years. And I've never had a complaint."

"Don't you mean you've never had a compliment?" Marty asked. Claudia gave him the claw.

"Why go?" Granger asked. "It's not mandatory."

She flashed a small pen recorder then stuffed it in her purse. "So I can get Patch to confess. He'll talk to me when he hears the trouble I went through to see him. I can be very convincing, you know."

"Unbelievable," Granger said.

"Thanks."

WHAT DO YOU WANT ME TO SAY, Molly?"

She dried her tears, wishing he'd hold her hand again. "Patch, I can't go through with this unless I know where we stand."

"We're friends."

"Who? You and me . . . or you and Erin?"

"No time for this," Patch said. "Look, in less than an hour the music starts. Then we're all paraded out in our best clothes. They prance us around like pet ponies. From what I've heard, there's food, speeches, clapping, and awards."

"Then cleanup. You told me."

"That's when we've got to be hiding outside and ready. Or we miss our chance."

ALL WE CAN DO IS WATCH?" After centuries the youthful angel was finally getting the picture.

"For now," the Shining One said.

"But we could help."

The Shining One held up his hands. "We will, but in God's timing. Not ours and not Patch's."

The smaller angel tapped his foot. "I hate being patient," he said, face glowing.

GIRLS ARE WEIRD." Marty spoke like an expert. They were playing after-school video games at the arcade.

"Claudia's kinda out there," Granger said, "but Nancy's not bad."

"Nan-see . . . Don't tell me. Please. Not her."

"What's your problem?" Granger said.

"She's into some scary stuff."

Granger poked Marty's shoulder. "Knock it off," Marty said.

"I'm trying."

"What?"

"That thing . . . It's sticking out his tongue at me."

Your support of New Peace Clinic has made this success possible." The back-patting speeches went on and on. Patch and Molly clapped at separate tables.

"Your blah, blah support is so very blah, blah . . ." Patch mimicked. Others at his table laughed, surprised. An adult he'd never seen before gave him a warning look. He smiled and kept quiet. With escape so near he felt free already; he didn't care if the other kids realized that he could talk. He liked to be the center of attention. Bored, he scanned the crowd.

His eyes widened. Was that her? Impossible. Yup, it was. Ms. Strong sat up straight in a sea of slouchers. He scrunched down. What was she doing here?

The choir director told Claudia, "Thanks for making the effort, but you don't have to sing with us. Really. The stage is small and we have all the parts covered." Others nodded.

"Oh, no, I wouldn't want to let you down," she said. She noticed eyes rolling all around. "Well, if that's the way you want it. Could I at least watch? That way I could show my support."

The director beamed at his good luck.

Claudia looked over the bored faces, trying to find Patch.

34

Not bad," Mr. Wattington said when the choir finished.

"I've heard worse," Ms. Strong said.

"I've sung in worse." He smiled and spread a napkin on his lap. "Hope they hurry with the food."

"I can't believe it." Ms. Strong said. "There's Molly."

"You knew she'd be here."

"Yes, but I didn't think we'd be so close to the . . . inmates."

"Patients." Mr. Wattington touched the back of her hand with his fingers. "I'm sure she'll be happy to stay away from you as long as you do the same."

Where was he? Claudia walked past tables full of bored kids and adults. A typical overblown event.

Finally she spotted him. She moved along the far wall. Closer, closer. When this foolishness was over, she'd pounce. With everyone dressed up and on their best behavior, no one would object to two old friends talking.

And one of them would be quite rich if the conversation went as she planned.

"THIS SURE BEATS SINGING IN CHOIR," Granger said. The two were playing against the machine, each gripping a separate steering wheel. "Just you, me, and it." Granger pushed at Marty.

"I've had it with you." Marty took a swing. Granger ducked. "Always teasing me. Making me think I'm an idiot.

"You really can't see it?" Granger asked.

"See what?" Marty said, clawing at his neck.

THE APPLAUSE DIED and people pushed to exits. Patch hurried to a side door.

The loudspeaker blared a recorded voice: "Patients, please report to your rooms immediately." Patch knew that meant everyone had to be counted before lights out. He and Molly had less than twenty minutes to slip out with the crowd and meet in the parking lot.

"It's been too long." Patch felt firm fingers dig into his shoulder. He turned. Claudia. He couldn't think of anyone he less wanted to see.

"Hey, how're ya doin'?" Patch said, eyes flicking toward the thinning crowd.

"Great. Now that we have a chance to talk." She slipped closer.

"We don't. I'll be marked missing if I don't get to my room. Can't get into trouble."

Claudia grabbed his wrist and held firm. "Take a couple of minutes to talk with an old friend."

MOLLY COULDN'T BELIEVE IT. She tried to get Patch's attention from afar, waved her hand at him. She could see that Patch needed help. Should she wait for him or keep moving?

She would stick with Plan A. Get to the staff vehicles and hide. Patch would catch up. He'd have to.

She turned to go. And almost ran into someone. "Ms. Strong!" she blurted.

"So you've found your voice." Ms. Strong said, Mr. Wattington at her side.

"I'm doing much better. Thanks for getting me the help I needed." Molly sounded sincere even to herself. But what choice did she have?

Gotta go." Patch stood.

"Nancy says you're doing great."

"She does?" Patch had to find out what else she said.

"Oh, yes," Claudia said. "She told us all about you."

Never. Nancy wouldn't have. He didn't know what to say.

"She says you're planning to escape."

Patch stared stone faced. "Yeah, like that would be possible."

Claudia laughed and pushed him into a chair.

Marty simmered down when Granger bought him a burger and double fries at the food court. Afterward, the two stepped into the restroom to wash off the grease.

Granger saw it again, sitting there.

But Marty wasn't buying it. Granger tried to describe the thing. "Kinda slimy. Horns over the eyes. You know, your typical personal-sized monster."

"Why are you doing this, Grange? Thought we were friends." The creature shook its hips and leaped from shoulder to shoulder as if on a trampoline. Marty squirmed as if his shoulders ached.

Granger stared. "You don't believe me. You think I'm crazy, seeing things you can't."

The limber lizardlike thing slipped along Marty's spine, making his shirt lump then fall. Marty spun to face the mirror. "Just me in all my handsomeness. Guess you're just nuts."

W HAT ARE YOU DOING HERE, NANCY?" Claudia demanded. Patch saw his chance and stood.

"Volunteering," Nancy said. Erin stood nearby.

"Almost like a school reunion," Patch said. "Too bad I don't have a yearbook for you to sign." He wished he could talk to Erin alone. "Nice seeing you all." He waved, glancing at Molly caught in her own conversation. No time to wait. It was now or never.

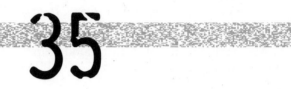

35

SORRY. I'VE GOT TO GO," Molly said. Ms. Strong pretended to act hurt.

Molly spun, took a step. Another roadblock.

Erin, Claudia, and Nancy stood in a tight line, arms crossed like security guards.

"We've missed you so much," Claudia said. "Love your hair." She reached to caress it, but Molly jerked away. "You don't have to be like that," Claudia said.

"I have to get going." The speaker again blared for patients to report to their rooms. "See?" Molly said.

"Good seeing you," Erin said.

"Almost sounds like you mean it."

Finally Molly was outside. Now to find Patch. She lifted her skirt and tore toward the meeting place.

TALK ABOUT WEIRD," Ms. Strong said.

"Maybe she didn't know what to say," Mr. Wattington said. "You two didn't exactly part as friends."

Ms. Strong glared, then softened and shrugged. "Wonder if she knows how Patch is doing. I should have asked. I've got to catch her."

Mr. Wattington strolled after her, then had to race to keep up.

PATCH PACED. Where was she? The van was there, wide open. This was their chance.

Someone was coming. He hid within the brush. But he couldn't leave without her. Not like last time with Amber.

"Told you it'd be worth our while." Two guys from the cleanup crew wheeled out tubs of coleslaw, strips of dry chicken, and plates of deviled eggs. "This will feed the fam for a couple of days." The two unloaded their haul, dividing it between the two vehicles. Patch crouched, watching.

The big barber came to the side of the van. He spoke to the men snagging snacks. "Sorry, guys. The boss sent me to tell you about the mess in the kitchen. Needs your help now." The men grumbled, but duty called.

So much for a ride, Patch thought. Oh well, Molly had ruined it all anyway.

He heard lips smacking. "This is good stuff." The man's mouth was full of deviled eggs.

Patch couldn't believe his bad luck.

SHE RAN THROUGH THE PARKING LOT, shoes slapping concrete.

"Molly? Molly!"

What now? Molly slipped between two cars. Ms. Strong chased her, and others followed, shouting her name. Molly covered her ears. Couldn't anything ever work out right?

114

*C*LAUDIA MARCHED BETWEEN THE VEHICLES. She banged them with open hands as she passed. Car alarms whined, roared, beeped. Patch came out of hiding and slid under the van and his shirt ripped. Feet stomped past.

What have you done, Molly?

His next thought was: *I don't know if I can help you. Not if I want to escape.*

*T*HERE YOU ARE." Molly looked up. Ms. Strong stood over her. "Thought you had to get to your room."

Molly opened her mouth, but words wouldn't come.

"Not that old mute trick," Ms. Strong said. "It's already been done."

Erin, Nancy, and Claudia, appeared. "Gotcha," Claudia said. Molly dropped her head into hands and sobbed.

Mr. Wattington herded the girls away. "Let Ms. Strong handle this."

Claudia pushed back. "Don't you dare try and cut me out! I want my piece. That reward's mine."

Molly noticed Erin and Nancy watching, the truth apparently dawning on them too.

*P*ATCH SLIPPED OUT FROM UNDER THE VAN, slid in the side door, and struggled past the food. He squeezed between the last two seats. Someone slammed the door, cranked the ignition, and floored the gas.

Molly would have to take care of herself.

Not my fault. Not my problem.

"So, Patch, where can I take you?" It was the big man, the tattooed barber. "Anywhere you want to go."

The plan was ruined now. Patch crawled out, swung into the passenger's chair. "You going to turn me in?"

"Nah, I'd never rat on a brother."

"What?" Patch looked over in surprise. The barber grinned and pointed at the tattooed arm nearest Patch. Patch locked onto the ink. He saw for the first time the battle represented on skin. A fight between good and evil, not just dragons and demons, but angels battling, swords slashing. "It's our secret sign. You know, Christians come in all shapes and sizes."

"But how'd you know about me?"

"My friend, the orderly, heard you talking with Nancy, scheming with Molly." Patch felt his face redden. He was glad it was dark. "Guess you're not as tricky as you thought."

36

Is Patch trying to make you one of his little Christ-Kids?" Ms. Strong said.

"I'm not sure what you're talking about," Molly said. She wasn't ready to turn Patch in, even if he had abandoned her.

"The Bible!" Claudia shrieked. "Does he talk to you about the Bible? Tell you about Jesus? Promise you heaven?"

"Ask him yourself," Molly said, pushing past Mr. Wattington. The others jostled to follow her back to the cafeteria.

God, protect Patch, she thought silently. Strangely, she expected an answer.

Look, I'm not describing it again. You already think I'm crazy." Granger sat in the emergency-care facility across from the mall. Marty had driven him there, forced him to see a doctor.

"Your dad has been called," the woman said.

"Great," Granger said. "What's going to happen to me?"

"I'm suggesting an appraisal at New Peace."

PATCH'S JAW DROPPED. "You're a believer?"

"Got that right." The two sat talking in the van like old friends. "Part of a larger group of renegades called the Tattooed Rats." The man drove slowly, sightseeing. "You never know when God's own will show up."

"Can we go back for my friend Molly?"

"If you want to get her in trouble too."

"What would you do?" Patch pulled on the seatbelt, tight across his chest.

"Turn myself in. Then pray first before trying something this crazy again. Just 'cause you see an opening doesn't mean you should walk through."

"You're right," Patch said. "Turn around."

YOU WANT TO BE LET BACK IN?" The man at the counter was frazzled. His pointy hair, tinted purple with silver highlights, looked brighter than he did. "Usually we're dragging you kids in here against your will. I'll have to find a supervisor."

"Just tell Dr. Max that Mr. Jones is back."

Patch still couldn't believe the barber was a Christian. And that sad-eyed orderly too. The tattooed man had given him directions to a group of believers who would welcome him if he ever got away.

"Trust only the Rats, man," the burly barber had said. "Not everyone who looks like a Christian can be trusted. Don't compromise what you know to be truth." The barber had parked the van a half mile from the clinic. Patch had insisted—he didn't want his new brother fired.

As he expected, Patch endured a long debriefing session. By the time he got back to his room, his clothes were torn and his face bruised. Apparently the staff didn't appreciate being embarrassed and had decided to teach him a lesson.

When Nancy and Erin came for their shifts the next day, Patch told them, "I came to my senses. I couldn't do that to Molly. We're friends."

He couldn't tell them about the mystery man with the tattoos. At least not yet.

"You care about her . . ." Nancy said.

Patch nodded. He touched the bridge of his nose. "Wonder if it's broken." Tears sprang to his eyes. He squeezed them out.

Molly burst into the room. "So it's true! I thought they were lying." She barely nodded at Nancy. "Why'd you come back, Patch?"

"I couldn't leave without you. I did that once. Never again."

Molly sobbed, clinging to his hands.

Nancy sat watching. "You almost make me believe you're for real."

"You know I am," Patch said.

*T*HE TRIP TO NEW PEACE WAS QUICK, QUIET. Granger had time to think and get even angrier. "You can't do this to me," he roared as he burst from the van. "I know my rights."

"You're delusional," Dr. Max said, oozing sincerity.

"But my dad—"

"Agrees you should be watched. Don't worry. We'll take good care of you."

*G*RANGER WAS TRAPPED, slumped over the sink, sick. His room had banana-yellow walls and no windows. A toilet perched in one corner, cameras stood behind protective glass in opposite corners. He was alone, but not alone.

I saw what I saw. Aren't we supposed to tell the truth? He could still picture Marty pointing at him with an accusing finger.

He flopped onto the bed, pulled the thin blanket to his neck, and closed his eyes.

He figured he should try to get some sleep.

37

T HAT'S RIGHT," THE SHINING ONE SAID. "He wasn't supposed to escape."

"But he could have made it."

"Doesn't mean he *should* have." The Shining One walked with his companion.

"What if he missed his only chance at freedom?"

The Shining One turned, flashed a knowing grin. "Guess we'll have to wait and see."

E RIN HAD INSISTED ON COMING with Nancy.

What a mistake, Erin thought now. If only she'd known.

She bounced from foot to foot. "I can't believe you're asking, especially with them here."

"Don't hide from the truth," Patch said. "Is it love or not?"

Erin was trapped. "What do you mean, 'love'?"

"We've talked about Jesus before, Erin. You seemed to get the picture." She nodded. Patch soothed the bruise on his chin. "And I've always wanted to ask you this: are you ready to make a choice?"

"I'm afraid." Erin hung her head.

Molly and Nancy stared open mouthed. "We all are," Patch said.

Erin was cornered. "Yes. I believe Jesus gave his life. Because he loves us."

"Then you know what you have to do."

Visitor for Patient 1210. Patient will report to the nearest care station."

"That's me," Molly said. As much as she wanted to hear what Erin would say, she had to find out who had come to see her. Maybe her parents? No longer angry?

But no. It was Ms. Strong.

"'Bout last night," Molly said. "Sorry."

"You were confused. I understand."

"You do?" Molly sat at the table across from Ms. Strong.

"Sure. We all go through times when we're not sure what's black, what's white, what's wrong, what's right. But you can make everything good again. Between you and your parents, your friends. Everyone. All you have to do is tell the truth."

The next morning, Granger awoke choking. Something squeezed his neck, laughed, then emitted an ear-shattering gurgle. He twisted toward the camera. "Don't you see it?" he rasped. But of course they wouldn't see it, and they'd be more convinced he was nuts. Anyway, the thing was already gone. Whew.

He scanned the room. The sink, the toilet . . . missing.

Then he knew.

He was still dreaming. Granger felt the claws at his throat, smelled the putrid breath in his face. He gasped. And as much as he shook, he couldn't pry the demon loose.

THE THREE TALKED ABOUT last night's excitement. "Maybe you two should be alone," Nancy said finally.

Patch shook his head. "Well, Erin?" he said.

"I believe it was love. Love brought Jesus to earth, love nailed him to the cross, love raised him from the dead. His love . . . saved us from our sins."

Nancy eyes widened. "Do you know what you're saying?" This went against everything she'd been taught. Everything she knew was right.

Erin turned to her. "Guess I'm a Christ-Kid too." Patch embraced her.

Nancy grabbed her purse. "I can't be part of this." Talking about Jesus Christ was illegal!

Without looking back, she left the room. She nearly plowed into Dr. Max. "Sorry," she said.

THAT'S ALL I'D HAVE TO DO?"

"You're a new person now," Ms. Strong said. "You even look different. Beautiful, actually."

Molly blushed. She had hoped someone would notice. Patch never did. She wanted to be clear about what was being offered. "So I tell you what Patch has been saying and I get back into school?"

"Of course."

But he *had* returned for her. On the other hand, he had left without her in the first place.

"He won't be hurt, will he?" Molly wondered aloud.

GRANGER COULDN'T MOVE. The writhing thing crushed his chest. His room was pitch-black except for two balls of light. Eyes. Granger pushed at the beast, trying to topple it. He was awake now.

He could draw only enough breath to cry out, "Help!"

"Trouble in room 12-C," a female voice announced over the PA system.

Suddenly Granger's room at New Peace was soaked in light. He lay on his back on the bed, feet flailing. Two attendants froze, seemingly unsure what to do.

The creature held Granger's shaking limbs. His chest stiffened, eyes wide open. He couldn't close them, couldn't move, couldn't make a sound.

Whats the problem, Nancy?"

"Doctor, I'm not sure what I should do."

"About what?" Dr. Max said.

38

B<small>Y THE TIME HELP</small>, including Dr. Max, reached Granger his breath was coming in slow, shallow gasps. "Get the paramedics!" a woman shouted. "Now!"

"Coma," the paramedic said when he arrived. "But look at his face. Like he saw something. Or thought he did. We've got to get him to a *real* hospital. Now."

Dr. Max ignored the slight and signed the paperwork for an emergency release via ambulance.

W<small>HY HIM?</small> Poor Granger." The apprentice angel wanted to yank the demons from the boy.

The Shining One restrained his assistant. "We're not on our own in this battle. God clears us for action or requires us to remain still."

"So what are we waiting for?"

"You'll see." The young angel pounded one fist into the other.

"In the meantime, learn patience," the Shining One said.

Jesus. Love. Christ-Kids." Dr. Max said. "Nancy, I can't believe you let it get this far."

He was right. She should have talked to someone sooner. But she hadn't thought it would get so serious.

"You're in trouble, young lady." His smile didn't match his words.

Nancy wished she could disappear. "I'll be happy to tell you everything I know." This didn't have to turn out bad for her. She cringed when she thought of Erin and Patch.

"Good, Nancy. I'll pull the digital recording from Mr. Jones's room. With that and your testimony, we should have all we need."

Molly watched her go. *Mistake!* She shouldn't have told Ms. Strong about Patch's notes, his explanations, the attempted escape. They were friends—at least they had been until Nancy and Erin stuck their noses in.

She hated to admit it, but Patch seemed to pay more attention to Erin and Nancy than to her. And frankly, she was jealous. So what if that was stupid; he had hurt her feelings. Well, at least she'd be getting out soon. That was all that mattered. Patch could fend for himself.

The loudspeaker called her to the nearest care station again. Another visitor? Already? Molly's smile returned.

39

I'M MOLLY." An orderly stood waiting.

"Come with me, please."

Molly hesitated. "Where are we going?"

"Back to an observation room."

"No!" Molly tried to pull free. "Not there again! Why?"

AFTER HER INTERVIEW with Dr. Max, Nancy sat in her car waiting, watching the clock. Thirty minutes . . . forty-five minutes . . . *I should just leave Erin, walk away from this mess. So what if she has to hitchhike home?*

Nancy looked up. "What's he doing here? He's not allowed out."

Erin and Patch stood at the passenger side window.

The speakers in the parking lot blared, "Patient John Jones has escaped. If you see him, call the New Peace operator immediately. Consider him armed and dangerous."

Nancy's laugh was hollow. "Yeah, you're dangerous. Now get back to your room before you get us all in trouble."

"I'm out," Patch said. "And I'm staying out."

"Then get in the car. Both of you. You attracted enough attention last night."

Erin slipped into the front seat, Patch in the back.

Nancy drove carefully toward the exit. A line of men stood, blocking their way.

LINDA STRONG FELT HER BLOOD PRESSURE CLIMBING, her face warming. She entered her password again. "Access Denied" flashed on the screen. Again and again. "You've got to be kidding," she muttered. Her students exchanged glances.

So close to claiming the reward and now she couldn't even log onto the World Peace Alliance Loyalty Processing Center website. She slammed her keyboard drawer shut and headed for Principal O'Connor's office.

He had to be behind this. No one else even knew.

GRANGER'S DAD TOUCHED HIS SON'S COLD HAND and pulled back at the coolness. The walls of the room matched his son's skin. The boy's unmoving eyes reflected the light overhead. The pupils were fixed and dilated.

"I'm sorry," he was told, "but we can only wait to see if he regains consciousness."

"How long?" The man stroked his son's forehead, pushed back a strand of hair.

"There's no way to tell."

"Do you think he'll come out of this?"

BACK AT NEW PEACE, Molly struggled to get her parents' attention. "Mom! Dad!" Molly slapped at the glass. "Please get me out! I'll talk! I'll be good!"

Her parents pointed and whispered.

"I'm better now!" They came closer. She couldn't hear a word, but she wanted to believe her mom was pleading her case. Her dad cocked his head, nodded.

The door clicked open.

"GET ON THE FLOOR," Erin said, yanking a bunched picnic blanket over Patch. She spun in her seat and fastened her seatbelt just as Nancy pressed the brake.

The uniformed man wore a gun. "Name," he said.

Nancy showed her volunteer badge. The man scoured his list. "Found it. Who's with you?"

"Erin Morgan," Nancy said.

"Yeah, both okay. Keep moving. You're blocking traffic."

40

I CAN'T STAND SEEING HIM LIKE THIS," the bent man said, holding his son's hand. "Grange, can you hear me?"

Nothing.

"Sorry, sir."

"Call me if there's any change overnight. I don't want him lingering like this. I'd rather let him die."

"We understand. You can fill out the preliminary paperwork."

Granger's father took one last look at his boy and let the tears come.

GRANGER HAD HEARD EVERY WORD. He struggled frantically to communicate, wanting to shout, to plead with his dad not to leave him.

Other beasts, dark and screeching, joined the torment. What were they? The putrid creatures hovered over his body, squeezing his wrists, covering his mouth, peeling back his eyelids. Immobilizing him.

Get off of me! Get off . . . Dad, can't you hear me?

"MOM. I'M HOME," Erin announced.

Terry scurried to her like a lost puppy. He clutched a plastic e-book. "Wanna read to me?"

"Later. Where's Mom?"

"Upstairs."

"Hi. Have fun volunteering?" Her mother took Erin's hand. "Maybe you didn't hear the latest on Granger. He's a friend, isn't he?"

MOLLY SANK INTO HER BED. It felt softer than she remembered.

She couldn't believe she was home. Tomorrow she'd be back in class. She stood at the mirror above her dresser.

"Wow. You do look good," she said smiling. On the ride home, her parents had told her they were proud of her, glad she finally told Ms. Strong the truth. They'd been in on the whole thing and had been waiting to see how she'd respond to the questions from her teacher. She'd passed the test, matured from this experience.

Molly had learned a lot. *Some good*, she thought. *Some not.*

With some weight off and a new haircut, she was a different person. New attitude too. She wasn't the same Molly who went on a speech strike, who caused disruptions in class, who talked about weird things with Patch.

She had changed. And she wanted everyone to notice.

41

"WHAT CAN I SAY, LINDA?" Principal O'Connor stood behind his desk, obviously determined to keep the meeting short. "Someone beat you to it. Sorry about your computer."

Ms. Strong wondered if she detected a smirk. "Who beat me? You know I've been working on this for weeks. I was counting on that new car. Certainly can't make that kind of money teaching here."

"Sorry, Linda. Sometimes things don't work out the way we plan."

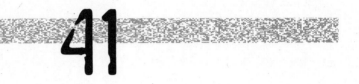

CLAUDIA PULLED MARTY ASIDE. "You hear? Ms. Strong got stiffed. Which mean we lost our part of the reward too!"

"That's supposed to be news?" He missed Granger. Marty's witty comments thudded without a buddy to bounce them off. "So who got the reward?"

"You'll never believe it," Claudia said.

I'M SURE WHAT YOU HAVE TO SAY IS IMPORTANT," Mrs. Morgan said. "But first, I thought you'd want to know that Granger has been hospitalized." Erin's face clouded. "Doctors don't know what to do."

Erin pictured Granger in her mind. Strong, tall, with a sweet smile. Nancy had been talking about him a lot lately. Wonder if she knew.

"Now," her mother said, "what was it you wanted?"

But Erin was already down the hall.

"Whenever you're ready, dear," Mrs. Morgan called after her. "I'm always here for you."

I HEARD, ERIN," Nancy said. "He could die tomorrow. His dad doesn't want him hooked up to some machine."

"Don't blame him . . ."

"How can you say that? He's our friend."

"Sorry."

"Isn't there anything we can do?"

"I'm not going anywhere near New Peace again . . . ever," Erin said.

"How's Patch?" Nancy said.

"Still hiding. Want to take him some food?"

"Yeah. Need to get my mind off Granger."

42

Ms. Strong spun as he passed without so much as a nod. She knew the latest fashion when it walked by.

Since when did he dress like that? He didn't know the first thing about style. A sweater from hand-spun imported angora. Beautiful at a distance, stunning at closer range. Fur taken from hand-fed rabbits that lived in rooms with piped-in classical music and videos of lush meadows to keep them calm. They were probably even asked permission before being shorn.

She'd priced one online for herself. Ridiculous. Astronomical. Plus new shoes. And slacks. The guy dressed like a model.

Ms. Strong watched from the window as he reached the parking lot, used a remote to start his vehicle, open the top, and roll down the window. A shining spotless convertible. Still had the dealer stickers on the window.

He wouldn't do that to her, would he?

HE GOT THE CASH," Claudia whispered.

"Who?" Marty asked.

"Wattington. He kept tabs on Ms. Strong . . . and us. All along he'd worked with someone at New Peace trying to get evidence against Patch and his sweethearts."

"Meaning?"

"Erin and Nancy are under suspicion too. And here's the best part: so is Ms. Strong."

"Never."

"My blabbermouth *friends* in the office said Mr. Wattington made it a condition of his reward."

HE AND HIS GUN WERE READY. The raid had been planned to the millisecond, the surprise to be complete. These two, Erin and Nancy by name, wouldn't escape.

Full names and physical descriptions flashed on his electronic readout.

He'd stun them, or worse, if he had to. Trained officers waited at every entrance to each of the girls' homes. "Suspects heading downtown," the headpiece crackled.

"Doesn't matter," the captain said. "Wait until they return and grab both at the same time. If they return to either residence we've got 'em."

SHE WALKED INTO CLASS and Marty took a step back. "Incredible, Molly."

"Thanks. Who'da thunk, huh?"

Molly knew she wasn't the same boring girl. Marty's googly-eyed response made her smile. She'd gone all out to make a statement, and her mom's credit card was still steaming.

"You look hot," Marty said. She could tell he approved.

"I know," Molly said.

"Can I carry your books?"

Molly laughed.

WITH THE MONEY SCROUNGED from the bottom of their backpacks, Patch had bought hair dye and thrift store clothes. He wanted to look like every other bored teen in town, wandering the park. He added magnetic earrings and henna tattoos.

"Over here," he shouted. He slipped the cheap sunglasses down. Erin and Nancy hesitated, then approached, slowly.

"That you, Patch?" Erin said.

Other teens clustered, smoking, pushing, chatting. Patch, Erin, and Nancy met at the statue at the center of the park. They sat on a picnic table beneath an elm. Erin and Nancy had details about Granger.

"We've got to pray," Patch said. The girls furrowed their brows and closed their eyes. "God," he began, "please help Granger."

"And God," Erin said. "Bring Grange out of the coma."

Patch's eyes popped open.

"Just show us You exist," Nancy said. "That'd be enough for me."

MAN WITH A GUN," the child said.

"Have you been watching the History Channel again?" his mother said. "You know guns are outlawed, silly."

"Outside." Terry pointed.

Mrs. Morgan peered out her back door and took a step back. "They must be here for Erin." *We never should have gotten involved with that terrible boy.*

She flipped open her cell and speed-dialed 2.

Pick up, Erin. Hurry.

43

Mom, I can't," Erin said. "I've got to go." She hung up.

"What's going on?" Patch said. Nancy leaned close.

"Mom says a team of WPA officers are outside my door. She wants me home."

"They're looking for me," Patch said.

"Or Erin," Nancy said.

"Or you, Nancy."

Nancy shook her head. "Think about it. This didn't happen until *you* started coming with me, Erin. You and I spent time talking with Patch . . ." Nancy shuddered. "You know what? This has gone too far. I can't jeopardize my scholarship chances." She ground a path, pacing. "My parents will be furious. We don't make waves. Ever."

"You're already involved," Patch said. "You know the truth."

"Stop it!" Nancy screamed. "You don't understand. I have my grades to think about."

"God will protect you," Patch said. Erin nodded.

"I don't want his help. I can take care of this myself."

THE SHINING ONE SHUDDERED as he saw Granger convulse. The towering angel sensed the demons' fear. They stabbed, poked, clinging, trying to hang on to the boy.

The Shining One and his helper yanked at the flapping, spitting burdens that weighed Granger down. At the touch of the angels, the shrinking creatures shrieked, hid in snatches of shadows. Granger was like a dog shaking off after a bath. He blinked, then opened his eyes. He lifted his hands. No claw marks, no bites. He opened his fingers and then made a fist.

"Hey!" he shouted. "They're gone! Can I get some breakfast?"

The door unlocked. *That's service.*

WHY'D THEY ATTACK HIM?" the less experienced angel asked.

"The boy was opening up to things of God, of the Spirit," the Shining One said.

"And the demons tried to crush him?"

The Shining One placed a hand on his friend's shoulder. "The devil ignores the kids who already belong to him."

WE CAN'T STOP HER," Erin said after Nancy left.

"It's her decision," Patch said. "What about you?"

"I'm calling Mom back. I need to tell her something."

EVERYTHING WOULD BE NORMAL AGAIN when Nancy reached home, everything fine when she stepped inside. When she pulled up and got out, she heard another car door open, but she refused to look.

"Nancy." She heard the voice but refused to turn. The lady called her again.

"Yes?" she said, pretending nothing was wrong. She stopped and turned to see a stout woman with a blonde ponytail. "I'm sorry, but I'm late."

From behind bushes at both edges of her house, officers ran. Four stood blocking her at the door.

Could they have found the other Bible?

"Come with us," the woman said. Nancy felt a hard hand on her shoulder. She could see her mother and father in the picture window. They already knew.

"Your mother packed your bag. Even your toothbrush."

Just like Mom.

"IT's YOUR DECISION, DEAR," her mother said calmly on the phone. "But you'll never see us again. Not that you seem to mind. I'll make sure you never see Terry again, of course."

"Mom, I know we don't always agree, but haven't you ever wondered if maybe there's more to life than life alone? Maybe God exists. Maybe he sent his son to save us. Maybe he cares."

"For your sake, I hope he cares. Because I don't."

NANCY'S STOMACH CHURNED as the van cornered quickly. Squeezed between two hefty officers, she was well padded from the bumps.

Logic wasn't helping and her confession to Dr. Max had backfired. He had turned her into the authorities. The traitor!

Erin and Patch were free, and she was trapped.

Life stinks sometimes.

All she had been trying to do was help out at the hospital, and look what happened. Maybe Mom and Dad would believe her, but they hated situations like this. Questions from neighbors. Everything had to be tidy.

She'd have to take care of herself.

At least she got her answer: *God doesn't exist after all.* Not for her, at least.

44

CLASS," Ms. STRONG SAID STIFFLY. "Let's all welcome Molly back."
The cheers swelled, punctuated by a few shouts. Molly didn't mind. She stood, spun like a model, and folded her arms into a yoga prayer pose.

THE WHOLE MORNING had done nothing to improve Ms. Strong's attitude. And now this. Ben trailing her like a puppy. "Linda, I couldn't help it. My mother needs surgery."

Ms. Strong stopped, fingered the collar of Ben's soft sweater. "Don't bother. You used me, used the kids . . . At least I was going to give them a cut of the money."

"Maybe, but I look great, don't I?" He spread his arms, showing off his look.

Ms. Strong pried the lid off her cafeteria coffee. Splash. His sweater sopped up every drop. Linda smiled at the storm forming on his face.

"You do," she said, "But I think you've got a small stain . . . right there."

45

BECAUSE SHE HAD FILLED OUT PAPERWORK TO VOLUNTEER, Nancy was already in the system. That made checking in as a patient a snap. She was assigned a room and renamed Jane Brown.

Real creative.

Her medication, administered via intravenous drip, was already working, her thoughts coming slower. Guess they'd learned their lesson with Patch. Nancy smiled. She remembered his barking routine with Dr. Max.

Speak of the devil. Here came Dr. Max with his clipboard. "I warned you about getting too close to the patients. Are you getting sleepy, Nancy?"

"Nancy? I don't know any Nancy." The drugs slowed her speech. "I'm Miss Brown. Jane's my name." She gave a goofy grin. "That almost rhymes."

"Very good," he said scribbling. *Weak-willed.*

Then Nancy saw someone familiar in the hall and things snapped back into place for a moment.

"Granger?" she said. "Grange!"

He pulled away from the man who held him around the shoulder and rushed into her room. "Nancy? What are you doing here?"

"Who's Nancy?" she said smiling. She remembered this guy. "Grange. I'm so glad you're okay. We prayed . . ."

"You what?" Granger said.

E̶RIN WEPT. "I can't, Patch. I love Terry."

He put an arm around her. "I know, so do I. But you can't go home now. They'll commit you." They rode a hydrogen-powered commuter bus, already miles from home, heading for the coast.

"Never see Terry again? I don't even have a picture."

"Hey, he's still here." He tapped his forehead. "And here." He patted his heart.

"What do we do?" Erin wiped her eyes.

"Find new brothers and sisters. New fathers and mothers," he said before slumping at her side for a nap. The ride would take several hours. They were headed to the address the orderly had given Patch—somewhere for Christ-Kids to hide.

T̶ALK ABOUT A FREAK," Molly said. "That guy was crazy."

"Forget Patch," Claudia said. "What was it like for *you* in that terrible place?"

"Oh, it wasn't that bad . . ."

Marty stood in the background. Several newcomers had pushed their way into the inner circle. The attention bolstered Molly's confidence, sharpened her storytelling.

"Have I told you about our escape plans?"

Marty had heard this part. He turned to go.

"Oh, Marty," Molly said, a smile in her voice. "How 'bout getting me another Slushie while you're up? Grape." She was back into her tale. Not even a thanks.

"Whatever you want," he said. He heaved his backpack over a shoulder and headed for home.

Nancy watched the fluid in the IV.

"You said something about praying," Granger said.

A smile started. "Jesus loves me, this I know . . ." Nancy was singing, her voice weak. A song she'd heard somewhere. "For the Bible tells me so . . ." She was fading, so sleepy. "Little ones to him belong. They are weak . . ." She was out.

What's she talking about?" Granger said. He didn't expect an answer. Dr. Max scribbled. Granger's father stepped in, looking as if he was afraid of catching something.

"Friend of yours?" his dad said, directing Granger out of the room.

"Yeah, but something's wrong with her."

This is it."

"It stinks," Erin said.

She and Patch had walked for blocks from the bus stop. Now they stood on a dirty dock off San Pedro Bay. A maze of slatted wood pathways crisscrossed nests of packing plants and encrusted fishing boats. The pier seemed to sway as the surf splashed at their feet. "This is what?" she said.

A hand-painted sign said "Sapiens Fisheries."

"Fishers of men," Patch said. "Time to eat."

Erin shook her head, exhausted. "Here? Gag me."

The stench of rotting fish wafted from the door, which hung cock-eyed on the rusting blue-and-gray metal building. It swung, clanging in the breeze.

"The Word's all we need."

"Whatever you say," Erin said, taking his hand. And they stepped inside.

46

"WHEW ... THAT SMELL," Patch said.

"You sure this is the place? Looks abandoned." Erin stepped nearer a small counter backed by a narrow aisle. Behind it was a large dark door. "Hope I didn't come all this way for nothing." She swooshed away the flies zooming at her eyes.

"If you felt that way, why'd you come?"

"Because I didn't want to get committed," Erin said. "Like you."

Patch shook his head. "So where's your faith? Or were you only pretending?" He slipped behind the counter, looking in cupboards, keeping busy. He wanted Erin to feel ignored.

"Don't accuse me of that, Patch. Remember, I'm new at this."

"Let's just try to find someone. This is where I was told to come."

Patch moved past stacked wooden crates, kicked away rotting fish heads. He used a small stylus to click on his stored maps on a handheld device. "Yep, this should be the place. I mean, the name on the sign is right. Sapiens Fisheries."

Patch banged around the storage space below the counter looking for a button or switch. "Should've at least set off some alarm by now."

Of course, nothing ever quite works for me.

The bulk of the warehouse stood behind the double doors. The steel clanged and echoed as he pounded.

"Patch . . ." He stopped and turned. "I've been thinking . . . a lot." Erin's hair hung in her eyes. "I should leave. Mom will get over this, and we'll be fine."

"Were you fine before?"

Erin made a face.

"It's up to you," Patch said.

"Hey, anyone around?" Erin called out, waving toward the creaking video camera panning the room.

ERIN GREW WORRIED. "Maybe we should force the door." She grabbed the handle and twisted. Her skin burned as she lost her grip. "Guess we're not welcome."

"Someone's gotta be here."

Erin crossed her arms. "Unless you're wrong again."

With a grinding screech the door swung open, forcing them into the waiting area on the other side of the counter.

A tall teen led a group into the lobby. "Discernment, thy name is Erin," he said.

Erin liked his smile. That and his longish red hair. Unruly though slicked back, it coiled at his neck. He looked like a lifeguard, lean and tanned.

"Name's Stan. Been expecting you." He ignored Patch, extending a hand to Erin. "Welcome, friend. We've taken it upon ourselves to become the official greeters since there are too many kids for the adults to keep track of."

Erin shook his hand, smiling. *Service at last.*

Stan's glance hardened when he turned to Patch, his hand now at his side. "Your reputation precedes you."

"Killer Kid," a ferret-faced girl blurted, then slid out of sight behind the others. The rest looked stony. Patch wanted to turn and run, but what could he say? They were right. He had exposed everyone he knew and loved to the wrath of the government. If he could take back that night he would. Amber would still be alive, and the others.

"So there's no compassion?" Patch asked. "No forgiveness for someone who made a horrible mistake?"

"You'll find some of those wimps here. Thankfully," Stan looked heavenward, "they're not in charge."

Erin cringed. "If these are your 'brothers and sisters,' I'd hate to meet the rest of the family."

SOMETIMES IT'S BEST TO GET OUT OF THE WAY," Ferret Girl said, emerging again. The short girl took Erin by the arm. "Stan and your boyfriend will work it out."

"He's not my boyfriend."

"Oh," she said dully. "Want to wash up? Get some food? My name's Cindy."

Patch watched the two slip through the door toward a hallway and a gaping entrance to a large room.

Stan and Patch faced each other.

Showdown time already?

"Three things you better remember," Stan said, staring at Patch. "We're watching you. I'm in charge. And the girl's mine now."

"You mean Erin? Doesn't she even get a vote?"

"Better than that. She'll think it was her own decision." Stan whacked Patch with the back of his hand, just hard enough to throw him off balance. "You want to survive, you'll listen, obey, and get on board. Above all, forget about the others."

"The others?"

"You don't want to even talk to them. You'll find a couple other clubs down here. This is the only one worth joining."

"And you're inviting me?" Patch said.

"I'm telling you to start begging. Maybe, eventually, I'll let you in. But whatever you do, avoid the Tattooed Rats."

On no, Patch thought. *I'm already on the wrong side.*

S O WE *DON'T* ALL LIVE HERE?" Patch said.

"That's old-think. Dispersing ourselves saves lives." The serious man sat behind a computer on a makeshift desk, a board perched atop two stacks of cinder blocks.

Patch was stunned. "No more hiding?"

Erin stood nearby. "We can stay?"

"*You* may, as our guest. Patrick is a problem." The man spoke as if Patch weren't in the room. "However, the elders have met and decided to put your friend on probation."

Patch could see his photo and text reflected in the man's enormous glasses. Then darkness. The man opened a cardboard box and took out two long, white envelopes. He handed one to each of them. "These will explain everything you need to know about where you'll be living and what your responsibilities are."

"What if I want to leave?" Erin said.

"Go ahead, miss. But know one thing: you'll never be allowed back."

"I can't believe he talked me into this."

Patch swung to face her, his face red. "You made your choice. You didn't have to come."

"I didn't have many options. Now I do."

"Knock it off." The man looked over the top of his glasses. "You two will grow up quick or die. There aren't enough adults around to baby-sit."

"Don't you want to try to fit in?" Patch asked. He looked to the man for support, but he was typing two fingered, tongue between his teeth.

"Not really," Erin said.

THEY WALKED TOWARD Erin's assigned housing together. Erin knocked. Patch stayed at the curb. A pudgy woman in her early twenties opened the door. A little girl, dark hair in a braid, held her mom around her knees.

"Are you one of them?" the mother said. She seemed to be waiting for Erin to sprout a tail or explode. "I'm not so sure this is going to work out."

Erin slipped inside. "Me neither."

"But I do want to offer my help," the mother said, reaching for Erin's envelope.

THE ELDER HAD TOLD PATCH that the believers met all together only for worship. "The rest of the time we're moving targets. You'll be pretty much on your own. Really teaches you to trust God." He smiled for the first time, several teeth missing. "Flush that envelope when you get to your assigned housing."

How come there was no mention of the secret sign the barber had told him about? Patch wondered about that. He thought he would have seen one of the Tattooed Rats by now. He almost asked about it, but something held him back.

Patch found the place where he'd be bunking, an old two-story house with a parched flowerbed and chunks of bricks missing from the facade.

From around the side of the house came a hunched man with baggy eyes and pitch-black hair. His face was as lined as a roadmap.

"I can find another renter with a snap of my fingers, young man. I'm waiting."

"For what?"

"I think you know."

This was like talking to Uncle Grant again.

"Can you give me a clue?" Patch said.

"Nope. No sir." The man—Mr. Sutherland, it said on the papers— spit tobacco into a circle of dead grass.

49

THAT EVENING ERIN RETURNED FOR WORSHIP, looking for Patch. Nowhere.

Then Erin spotted her: a scary-perfect blonde. Her shiny hair bounced. Her smile was large, her teeth white as marshmallows. And that tan. Flawless. Jealousy nipped at Erin.

Blonde Girl was heading her way. Erin wanted to run. The walking, talking Barbie doll hummed to a stop before her.

"We are *so* happy to see you."

Erin imagined the girl's head jangling like a bobble toy.

We? The girl stood alone.

"I speak for *all* the cool kids down here, of course." She waved and a clump of teens moved closer, an unbelievably perky crew.

They all looked too happy. "What's the joke?" Erin said.

Blonde Girl flipped her hair. "Nothing. We're on a new path, that's all." Her words didn't seem to match her expression. "The only one that brings peace and fulfillment. You're welcome to sit with our group. Everyone thinks we're pretty cool."

"Christians, huh?" Erin said. "Not interested."

"No one will force or badger you. Be a part of us, or don't."

"There's no wrong answer, then?"

"Right . . ." Blonde Girl smiled another impossibly large smile.

"I'll get back to you," Erin muttered.

This crew made Stan's gang look normal.

Ｐ**ATCH FINALLY FIGURED OUT** that Mr. Sutherland, his new landlord, was waiting for the envelope. He handed it over.

"This place has been in the family for three generations," the old man said. "Not fancy, but it'll do." Mr. Sutherland was tall with a hump to his back. "Especially for the likes of you."

The man shredded the seal and flipped through the papers. "That'll buy you a bed and light meals for the month. And stay out of the kitchen. The fridge will shock anyone trying to get an extra snack."

"So three-minute showers, eat in my room, never pick up the phone, stay away from the windows, leave the dogs alone, don't switch cable channels, and keep my mouth shut. Is that all?"

The man grinned and his face crinkled like an old newspaper. "For starters."

Ｙ**OU JUST MET TIFFANY,**" Stan said. "If you're unlucky you'll meet the Rats later."

Erin laughed. "Can you say 'Barbie'?"

"I'm surprised Tiffany and Company have managed to keep themselves fed and clothed this long," Stan said.

"But they're Christians? You're Christians? Very different brand, I'd say."

"The others don't know the first thing about being believers. We do. For us, it's not just 'anything goes, believe or don't believe, whatever you want.'"

"How do you know you're the ones who've got things figured right?" Erin said.

50

Patch stopped in at the tattoo shop. Patterns and possibilities covered the walls. He couldn't believe he was doing this. Many of the graphics were scary, wicked. He almost turned to go. Nah, this wasn't him. It wasn't going to work. But he didn't have a choice, at least not according to his friend, the Tattooed Rat at New Peace.

If he ever hoped to be accepted he had to take a tat. That simple, that clear. So that's what he was going to do. When the Rats were ready to make themselves known he'd know somehow.

For now he was going to trust the advice he'd gotten was accurate even if it seemed a little crazy.

A short, brown-haired girl squinted at him. "Ever had one before?"

"No."

"It hurts."

"Great."

"What kind do you want?"

"Something small. Like that." He pointed.

"Not another one."

Patch pulled down his sock to just below the ankle. Half an hour later he left with a small, plain fish embedded in his skin. Nothing showy, but enough to prove his loyalty to the Tattooed Rats, the group he'd been sent to join. Nice thing was he could cover it when necessary.

E RIN WASN'T IMPRESSED. "So it can be tiny? The whole thing seems weird to me. Who'd want to be a part of them? They don't have a very good reputation."

"You'll have to make your own choice. But I sure wouldn't take the sign unless you mean it." He pulled his sock up. "It's an ancient symbol for those who followed Christ, you know?"

"Actually, I didn't, professor." She glared at him, tired. "Would you let me make my own decisions?"

"What's wrong?"

"I miss Terry. And my parents. Of course, you wouldn't understand."

"My family's gone too," Patch said.

"Yeah, I know. Sorry." Maybe he was right. If only these shadowy Rats would show themselves, that might help clear things up for her.

P ATCH MET THE TATTOOED RATS FIRST. Gary was outside the coffee shop. His drawings covered his arms from wrist to shoulder. The sleeveless tank made it obvious that he was proud of his arm art. Patch had never seen anything like it.

Gary's gray eyes grew grim. "You were warned, weren't you?"

A crowd gathered. Everyone wore black, or dark solid colors. Patch had never seen so many tattoos. The mass squeezed him like a constrictor at mealtime.

"Didn't you hear me?" The big man, Gary, stepped closer and flexed a bicep. "See the fishy?" Patch thought it looked more like a whale. He was right.

"So?" Patch had no clue.

"I thought you were a Christian."

"I am," Patch said.

"Then you should recognize Jonah," Gary said.

Patch looked closer. The huge mammal had a human head and shoulders poking from its mouth. And the guy was waving! Patch laughed.

"When they said we had to take a fish tattoo, I took it to the extreme."

Patch looked closer and saw Abraham and Isaac, Noah and the Ark, entwining leaves, and Celtic crosses. *Impressive.* He pulled down his sock to expose the one-inch line drawing of a fish. The muscle man leaned over, waved the others nearer.

"Awesome," Gary said, giving a thumbs-up.

Others patted Patch on the back. Amid murmurs of encouragement and congratulations, Patch began to belong.

It had been a long time.

51

THE SHINING ONE WATCHED PATCH head toward the glass-paned door of the coffee shop. Rented by undercover Christians, the run-down place served as a meeting place for believers. Until Patch was trusted enough to be told of the worship times in advance, he'd have to settle for the coffee shop for all his updates.

"Any action planned?" the assistant angel asked.

"Not at present. Wait and be ready."

PATCH RUBBED A WARM SPOT at the back of his neck. A presence? Was someone watching? He looked around. An older couple walked toward him, kids on bikes yelled.

Maybe he was wrong.

Again.

Tiffany was in the coffee shop. She stopped talking when Patch walked in. He waved to her. She smiled. "So your friends all died, huh?"

Nothing like a warm welcome. He nodded.

"No way you could have helped?"

"By not being born."

"Get over it," Tiffany said. "Agree it was no one's fault and move on."

Easy to say if it wasn't your fault.

Someone pulled out an empty chair. He sat.

"What was it like being in a raid?" a freckle-faced boy wearing a baseball cap said.

Patch just shook his head.

"Forget that," Tiffany said. "If Patch wants to move on and forget the past, we should respect his decision."

Freckles shrugged. "No pressure."

A tall girl with straight hair sat across from Patch. "Exactly. There's nothing wrong with getting along. If we'd try it more often, maybe we wouldn't be such outcasts, always hiding. Always scared."

"You've got to be kidding!" Patch said. "For years Christians tried to get along, play by the rules, fit in. All it got us was rejection. We were interfering with the WPA and its smooth order of business." He scratched his ankle.

"Yeah," a voice said, "and that got many of us killed."

"Spoken like a true Tattooed Rat," Tiffany said.

Gary and a couple of his guys had entered. When one went to the counter, the tattooed hulk looked at Patch and pointed toward the open seat next to him.

Patch sighed. Another choice. He stood to take his place with the Tattooed Rats. Tiffany made a gasping-fish face.

Erin popped in with Stan, his arm around her waist. They breezed past, parking at the last empty table. Stan bowed his head. Erin caught Patch's eye and winked.

52

S*O THIS IS POPULARITY.* Molly took a deep breath and waved at another would-be best friend. The last couple of weeks had flown by.

Claudia scurried up. "Hey, Molly. Wanna get a pizza tonight?"

"With you?" Molly's new-found cheekbones pulled taut.

"No, I was going to let you eat alone."

Molly smiled. "Ouch. Too busy tonight. Later, maybe?"

P*ARTY TONIGHT!"* Claudia whacked away at the exclamation point till a dozen streamed across the screen. She hit "Send" to almost everyone she knew. Except Molly.

"Will b there." Marty shot back instantly. "Will the Queen b there 2?"

Claudia and Marty also called Molly Miss Prissy Princess behind her back.

"She's simply swamped . . ." Claudia typed. Then added, "Miz Strong isn't happy with her either."

"Cuz?"

"Hasn't learned to shut up yet."

"So unlike us. We never speak unless spoken to."

When Molly had returned from New Peace she wanted to hang in the back with the cool kids, but they never listened in class. And she wanted to.

Molly now wore the right clothes. But she cared about more than looking good. She wanted to learn. Funny. She was finally welcomed into a group she didn't want any part of.

"You going?" A girl leaned over to let Molly read the message from Claudia.

"Sorry," Molly said. "Studying." She knew what Claudia was up to.

When Ms. Strong strode past, Molly sat up straighter. She patted her backpack and felt the hard bump of her journal. Her lifeline. The only friend she had left.

In it she asked herself questions that weren't allowed anywhere else. And she actually tried to answer them. After a day of brainwashing, her mind needed exercise. Journaling gave her space to think.

Sometimes in class, Molly felt like a balloon being pumped with yet more hot air. Something had to give.

"Who's read their homework?" The buzzing stopped. Ms. Strong peered around. Molly shook her head. The question always seemed foolish to her. "Problem with that, Miss Molly?"

"Guess I don't see the point of trying to sort the liars from the scholars. The only way to know for sure is to ask a real question." Molly turned to a boy. "I'm sure Robby did his reading. Just like me." The long-legged boy blushed.

"Did you do your assignment, Rob?" Ms. Strong said.

"Like always."

The class roared and Molly egged them on.

"Enough!" Ms. Strong stomped as she paced.

What a waste. Day after day of nothing. Nothing new, nothing tough. For the umpteenth time Molly wondered what Patch was doing. Where was he?

Molly raised her hand at the next question, and though she looked like a model, she spoke like a student who'd scoured her books.

53

ONLY A HALF DOZEN KIDS SHOWED UP to Claudia's party, and she was irritated at how much they ate without paying.

No good snubbing Molly if she doesn't show up.

Marty and Claudia were the only two left, sipping root beer through a straw.

"She's about to tumble," Claudia said. "And we'll be there to take her place."

"You're still jealous 'cause Patch liked her instead of you. Come to think of it, he liked everyone better than you."

"Tomorrow still okay?" she said.

"Yeah. But I doubt she'll buy it."

"Just do your part. Leave the convincing to me."

"CAN YOU BELIEVE IT?" Claudia said in the crowded hallway. "I never expected to hear from Patch!" She knew Molly was close enough to hear. "Can I trust you, Marty?"

He nodded and the pair pretended to be whispering. Suddenly Molly stood over them.

"Hey, guys."

Claudia looked up and raised her eyebrows.

"Did I hear you mention Patch?" Molly said.

"Tell you after class. I need to review my homework first."

Molly felt like screaming. Why couldn't she ever play the game? Act like everyone else? And as for Patch. She couldn't believe it. He should have trusted her, not Claudia. Didn't make sense. Of course, maybe she didn't understand Patch like she thought she did.

Class was about to start. She spun around to hurry to her room, and she saw him, a handsome guy she'd nearly run down. *Wow!* He gave her a strange smile and walked away. "Didn't catch your name," she said to herself. "And probably never will."

MOLLY JUST WANTED TO GET HOME AND PULL OUT HER JOURNAL. But Claudia and Marty blocked her path. "Thought you wanted details."

"I do. How is Patch?"

Claudia glanced around like she was doing a spy sweep. "Guess it's okay to talk. You two *were* good friends. He misses us and says he's fine. Erin too."

"That's it?"

Claudia pretended she was wracking her memory.

"Not much of a message," Molly said. "Thanks anyway." Molly bounded down the school steps. A guy buzzed past on a solar scooter. Same guy she'd seen in the hall.

Wow!

SEEN GRANGER YET?" Claudia opened her eyes wide. She loved being the first with the latest gossip.

"He's out already?" Marty said.

"Got a suspended sentence for good behavior." Claudia rolled on some more lipstick. "I'm sure we'll see him around soon. But be prepared."

"For what?" Marty looked concerned. Claudia snapped her compact closed.

"He doesn't look like the Granger we remember. His eyes are different."

"Huh?" Marty had no idea what she was talking about.

"He's scared, acts like someone's waiting to jump out at him behind every corner."

"He misses my jokes, that's all."

Claudia shook her head. "I'm sure that's it."

WHEN THE HANDSOME GUY saw Molly he skidded to a stop, waved her over. He introduced himself and folded up his lightweight scooter, flung it over his shoulder.

"I'm Trevor Melina," he said. "Okay if I walk you home?"

She smiled. There was nothing she'd enjoy more.

On the way the two discussed everything: pets, classes, scary teachers they'd had. Molly found herself listening a lot, feeling comfortable. She noticed his dark eyes were clear. Very confident. She liked that in others because she didn't feel it in herself.

The two of them walked on. The topics had gotten deeper.

"Won't do me any good now," he said, "and besides, I'm not worried 'bout tomorrow."

Molly shrugged. "So you don't ever think about dying?"

"If it happens, it happens. That's it. All over."

"Heaven's probably too much to hope for . . ." Molly said.

Trevor adjusted the scooter. "If it existed I'd boycott it. I avoid deities that exclude good people."

"I hear heaven is a reward."

"Sounds more like a club. If I had to give up the things I love"—He looked Molly in the eye—"or the people I care about, I wouldn't call that paradise."

WANT TO COME IN?" Molly liked this guy.

Trevor held up a hand while he checked his cell. He read a text message, then said no. Without a word, he pounded down the porch steps, reassembled his scooter, and tore away, backpack over his shoulder.

Well, at least he walked me home. An actual conversation with a guy. That was a change. And he was smart too. Everything had been going great until he got that message.

Maybe it's me.

She hadn't been inside ten seconds when urgent pounding came from the door. Had Trevor forgotten something?

Ugh! It was Claudia. "Surprise! Tell me all about him! I want to know everything!"

"We just talked. He didn't tell me much about himself."

"No one knows anything about him," Claudia said. "And his records are sealed. I checked. He just appeared this week."

56

THE NEXT DAY, MOLLY WATCHED TREVOR, DECIDED TO GET CLOSER. He was on his cell phone. "I'll find out," she heard. "Stop worrying."

"Find out what?" Molly said.

He turned slowly, snapping the phone shut. "Eavesdropping a hobby?"

"Sorry," she said. "Just teasing."

With short blond hair and midnight-blue eyes, the young man was almost exactly opposite in appearance to her. She liked the contrast.

"Want to grab lunch?" he said. Molly smiled.

DURING HER NEXT BREAK BETWEEN CLASSES, Molly stood in the hallway. She almost felt like heading home, pretending she was sick. But then she heard a voice. She knew it. "Granger? Is that you?"

He looked different. Molly couldn't explain it. Something was wrong.

"Great to be back. Don't want to visit that place again."

"I know *exactly* what you mean." They stopped along the wall, ignoring the crowd, the laughter, the noise.

"Have you seen them too?" Granger said.

"Who?" Molly said. She wouldn't meet his eye.

"Never mind." Granger leaned against the wall and blew out a long breath. "Still tired, I guess. Heard anything from Patch?"

Was this some trick? "Later, Grange. I need to do something before class."

TREVOR TOOK THE SEAT beside Molly.

"I ended up getting my classes switched," he said. "Weird, huh?"

Her geometry teacher blathered about triangles, and Molly tuned out. She usually enjoyed this stuff, but she couldn't focus today.

Trevor tapped away with his stylus and raised his eyebrows at her. He grinned.

Something about him was not quite right. What was it? He almost didn't look real, reminding her of figures she's seen in a wax museum. As she studied him, a long black tongue shot from his mouth and flickered inches from her nose. She jumped up screaming.

"Molly!" the teacher said. "What's the matter? Sit down!"

"But, but— He . . ." She pointed at Trevor, who sat there looking normal, except for a confused expression. His wide, sparkling eyes looked at her with wonder and concern.

She was the one acting crazy.

57

"GUESS WE CAN'T KNOW WHAT LURKS behind those big brown eyes," Claudia said. "Maybe she's got problems we don't know about."

"Hope so," Marty said. Claudia gave a half grin.

"So how are you?" Trevor said, joining them. He put a hand on Claudia's shoulder and the other on Marty's. He pushed hard, and Claudia smacked his hand. He released them.

Claudia looked over his shoulder. "Oh, Molly," she said. "Got something for you."

"That's why I'm here," Molly said.

"Something wrong?" Trevor said, eyes shimmering.

Molly looked away. "Overtired. That's all." She took the printout from Claudia.

Must meet, soon. Will send details through my friend, Claudia. Please don't let me down again. Patrick.

MOLLY LOOKED AT HER without blinking. "Thanks, Claudia. You've always been there for me . . . and now for Patch." Lying was coming easier. She felt like a bird caged with a pack of starving cats.

But she knew. That note was clearly a phony. Patch would never have called Claudia "my friend." And he would have signed it "Patch," not "Patrick."

Molly was glad she had her journal. A place to spill her soul.

GRANGER BANGED ON THE DOOR. Nancy's mom opened it a crack. "Yes?"

"I'm Granger, a friend of Nancy's."

"Please come in. She's very sick. Has been for some time." She gestured to the long hallway on her left. "Sleeping right now."

"Oh, she was released?" Granger said. He didn't get it.

"What are you talking about?"

"You mean she's out of New Peace?"

TALK TO ME, MOLLY."

The nerve. She couldn't believe he dared sit next to her.

Trevor ate his sandwich, chomping loudly like a dog with a bone.

"What happened in geometry?" she wanted to know.

"That's what I was going to ask you. You sure seemed upset." His eyes sparkled.

Maybe she had imagined the whole thing. "What's wrong with your tongue?"

Trevor hooked each corner of his mouth with a forefinger and wagged his pink, ordinary tongue like a kid at the dinner table.

Molly pushed her meal toward him. "Lost my appetite," she said.

58

I DON'T GET IT, CLAUDIA," Granger said. "Why would her mother refuse to admit Nancy's been hospitalized? Don't they want her to get better?"

"Forget Nancy," Claudia said. "Stop asking questions. You're better off without any ties to her."

"Right now answers are the only things I'm interested in. Maybe if you went with me, her mom would open up."

Claudia bit her lower lip as if actually considering. "Nah, I've got other things to do."

Granger felt quick anger prick him. What did Claudia have against Nancy?

"Well, I'm going to find out." He stood.

"Your decision. It's your time to waste." Claudia said.

REVOR'S EYES FLICKERED. "I've got to go. Found out we have an infestation problem at the house. In my bedroom."

"That tongue of yours should clean up the bugs in no time." Molly couldn't believe she'd said that.

"And yours will get you in trouble," Trevor said, leaning close. "Big time." He yanked the zipper on Molly's backpack and snatched her leather-bound journal. Papers, pens, and books hit the ground as he ran.

Y**OU'RE BACK**," she said coldly. "What now? Nancy can't have visitors."

"I want to know more about her," Granger said. "I care about her."

Her mother nodded slowly. "We'll talk on the porch." Granger followed her to a pair of oversized rockers. "Sometimes even a parent doesn't understand things," she began. "I used to think I had all the answers. Now I'm sure I don't."

Granger didn't know what to say, so he listened.

"She's been such an embarrassment to us." She pulled a Kleenex from her pocket.

"I think she's wonderful," Granger said.

"She was . . . once upon a time. Before she brought those things to our home." She shuddered.

Granger looked at her in surprise. He thought he knew just what "things" she was talking about.

O**PEN UP, T**REVOR!" Molly said, banging on his door.

Every secret thought, every confusing question had been poured out on those pages.

A man answered the door. "Hello, miss. I'm Trevor's father."

"I need to talk to him."

"He's out tonight. With friends." The man looked like a generic dad clipped from a clothing catalog. Seemed like she'd seen him before. His black but graying hair was short with a few tufts over his forehead. Didn't look much like his son, she thought.

Molly let out a breath. "Please tell him Molly stopped by. He borrowed a book of mine and I need it. Please."

On her way from the house Molly slipped behind a tree. A window was open, so she listened for any evidence Trevor might actually be home.

"I thought you were trying the good-guy routine on that kid," Trevor's father said. "You got her mad."

"It was worth it. Look at this diary. Lots of leads on that Patch kid. Erin too."

Molly crept to the window and peeked in. Trevor was there, with his dad. As she watched they slipped out of the coverings that made them look human, and there stood two dragons—demons, horned beings. As they conversed their tails twisted on the carpet.

"She'll lead us right to him."

W*HY GOD?*

Why am I seeing this evil? Why am I the only one? Or am I the only one brave enough to admit it? Molly scribbled in a new notepad, the words coming almost faster than she could get them down. She wanted to recreate her journal, tried to remember every word she'd written. She'd said so much about Patch, Erin, Nancy, and her own time in the hospital. And she'd slipped in the new note about Patch wanting to meet with her. It was fake, but still . . .

Dare she write what she had seen at Trevor's house? No one would believe her. She'd be judged insane, sent back for more *treatment.* That she would never allow.

T*HE* DAYS CREPT BY for Nancy. *I don't have a choice,* Nancy kept telling herself. *I don't have a choice.*

So she spewed the standard responses: "Tolerance is truth. Friends are family. War is always evil."

"Good work, Nancy," Dr. Max said, beaming. "I think you're ready."

"Only if you're sure, Doctor." Nancy said, her voice strong. "I don't want to shame my family again."

"You're nearly healed," the physician said, sitting back and folding his arms. "I can tell."

Nancy's parents had presented the mobile she'd made for Mr. Wattington's class as evidence of her illness. Proof she was crazy. As Dr. Max rambled, she studied the mirrored faces twisting above her and wondered if she'd ever be well.

I DON'T BELIEVE IT, STAN," ERIN SAID. "Patch wouldn't do that."
They were talking over coffee. "I trust him. I can't explain it any better
than that."

"Then why aren't you sitting with him?" Stan crossed his arms,
started flirting with another girl. Erin squirmed.

THAT'S ALL," THE OLD MAN SAID. "Nothing to it." The left side
of his face drooped from a stroke. Patch studied his earnest, twisted smile.

"Sounds simple." He put his back in to the work, carrying the bagged
fruit from collection carts. Exhausting. But he wanted to help. He saw
no other way to improve his reputation. No one offered a hand.

That was okay with him. "Better than an exercise machine," he said
to himself. The apples were heavy and sweet smelling, like fresh cider.

Anyway, I deserve this.

As Patch worked, Stan and Erin entered the warehouse, early for
the worship service. Stan pointed. "That's what I like to see. The wicked
working out their punishment with fear and trembling." He rubbed his
arms and faked a shiver. "Let's see some more fear and trembling."

"Need some help?" Erin said.

"Sure, thanks," Patch said.

"Not allowed," Stan said. He grabbed Erin's wrist. "C'mon. The meeting's about to begin."

Left out again. Fine. Patch would show everyone that he never gave up.

The old man hobbled toward him, left leg dragging. "Good work, son. Let's get to the service."

Patch heaved a last bag onto a pile. It split open and apples rolled. "Leave 'em," the man said. Patch wiped his hands and followed the crowd into the warehouse.

It looked like heaven. Sweet singing, peaceful faces.

Stan stood near the front with his hands clasped. He could have passed for an angel. Erin stood at his side.

R̷OTTEN." Stan spit out the apple. He examined another and smashed it to the floor.

"Didn't he check them first?" Ferret Girl said, nose twitching. Erin hung her head at Cindy's nasty words.

"What's going on?" Patch said.

Oh no, Erin thought.

"You're the problem," Stan said pointing. "They're all ruined."

"What are you talking about?"

"The apples you moved to the storage area were already fermenting. So you destroyed the rest. So no applesauce for the babies, no dried slices for the rest of us." Stan shook his head. "Why didn't you look into the bags? Didn't they smell a little too sweet to you? Ever hear the expression 'A bad apple spoils the bunch'?"

"I'm sorry. I didn't think—"

"Again." Stan held up a hand. "We all make mistakes. I'll talk to the elders about giving you another chance." He looked at Erin, his face gentle.

What a nice guy, she thought.

"Not that you deserve it," Ferret Girl said, and she scurried away.

GOD, PLEASE. WHAT'S WRONG WITH ME?" Patch was alone in his room, praying in the darkness. "I'm sorry. I deserve everything Stan can dish out, but I'm begging you . . . please help me." When he opened his eyes he felt better. He believed this was all part of God's plan to punish him. His decisions had cost Amber, Grandma June, Uncle Grant, and the others their lives. He felt so alone.

He would never make excuses again. No more explanations, no more reasoning, or trying to talk his way out of trouble. He would do what God wanted him to and take the consequences. If people misunderstood, so be it.

It was time to grow up.

STAN'S EYES BLAZED. "How dare you question me, Erin? You now know all the details; nothing has been kept from you. Being a friend to both Patch and me won't work."

"He was there for me," she said. "You don't know how he came back for his friend, the way he treated my little brother . . ." She was tired of explaining.

"You're my main concern," Stan said. "I don't care what happens to him." He put his hand on Erin's but she pulled away. "Can't you see how I feel about you?"

Erin looked away.

"Unless you select the right side," he said, "you may be left outside. You belong with the winners."

"Or else I'm a loser?"

ERIN HAD TO THINK, get away from everyone for a while. She took a long walk, watched the white gulls gliding and diving near the beach. After an hour she knew she could handle another round with Stan or Patch. Whoever she happened across first.

How am I supposed to choose between them?

She wondered what to do. She entered the coffee shop. *A double mocha always helps.*

Stan and his group bowed their heads. His voice was strong, deep. "Oh, heavenly Father, give us your wisdom. Help us see past the masks and understand your truth." The words lulled Erin, making her feel as safe and warm as when she curled up in the big chair in her living room. She thought of Terry tumbling on the floor, begging to be tickled. She missed him.

Maybe Stan was the real deal. He certainly looked it. And that calming voice. She moved closer. When the prayer ended, she stood waiting. For him. She had decided.

Stan pulled out a chair for her and snapped his fingers. Someone rushed to get her a coffee.

62

"How can you defend the guy?" Gary was getting louder. "He cuts you down every chance he gets. Blames you for putrefying the pantry with rotted fruit. Tells lies behind your back . . ."

"I'm not one to throw stones," Patch said.

"Or apples," Gary said, smiling and crossing his arms so his tattoos bulged. "I like your attitude. It's weird, but something tells me you're heading the right direction."

Gary and Patch strode down an alley where Ferret Girl stood talking to a Tattooed Rat. They had their heads together, whispering. Cindy pointed toward Patch and scurried away when they approached.

"What was she saying?" Gary said.

The girl gulped. The tattoo on her wrist showed roses in bloom, a fish-shaped figure etched into the center of each flower. She made a face at Patch. "She told me what he did." She refused to speak to Patch.

"You believe her?" Gary said.

"Gotta run." The young woman hurried off.

"You're in trouble, Patch," Gary said. "That girl's a believer, but she keeps a secret only long enough to tell someone else. It's not nice, but we call her the Gossip Queen."

Erin paced. "You know you're being accused of everything from murder to poisoning the stew, Patch." Erin put a hand on his shoulder. "I didn't want to believe the stories. I thought I could trust you."

Patch shrugged.

Erin looked down.

"Stan's behind the rumors, you know," he said. "Ugh! I've said too much." He had promised himself he would not explain, not blame, not tear down. But he desperately wanted Erin to understand. She was a friend.

"Enough, Patch." She held up her hand and stepped back.

63

PATCH WALKED SIDE STREETS AND CRISSCROSSED ALLEYS. He felt a chill in the night.

"God, I'm back," he said. "Tired of me yet? I don't know what to do. Leave and give Erin a chance without me? I'm sorry for what I've done to Amber and the others. But you know that, God. You already know." He leaned against a building.

THE SHINING ONE STOOD NEAR, THRILLED. His companion felt the surge of power sweep over them. The message true and clear.

The young angel wanted to fling off his heavy jacket, run to him, offer kind words. Patch sounded so sad, so weary. But he had to remain still, secret.

That was his role and responsibility. Stay in position. Remain ready.

The young angel closed his eyes as the prayers crashed heavenward.

WE MUST DECIDE WHO WE CAN BELIEVE. I personally have seen Stan's good fruits. You know where I stand." The man leading the meeting wore a neatly trimmed brown beard. His eyes were sad. "But please. Any other comments?"

"I think he's right," the woman said, gesturing to the speaker.

The man who'd had the stroke tried to explain. "I feel in my spirit that Patch can be trusted." It was hard for him to speak. "He seems so earnest, always pitches in." The others ignored him.

"Something must be done or the influence will spread," said another elder. "Those Tattooed Rats are the problem."

"Even if we agree Patch has turned over a new leaf, he's become involved with those who refuse to follow our plans and programs. They want to do everything their own way. And you know what that means." The woman looked down at some notes. "Stan has explained what they're really up to. They want to undermine his honest efforts."

"It's decided, then," the bearded man in charge said. "The welcome mat has officially been rolled up for anyone who identifies with the Tattooed Rats. I'll make the announcement tomorrow at worship."

"IMPOSSIBLE," Gary said. "Are you trying to be more spiritual than Stan? Than Jesus himself?"

"No," Patch said. Misunderstood again. "If God put the thought in my mind, he'll give me the words. Or help me keep quiet. I'll let God defend me."

Gary shook his shaggy head. Dark outlines of Bible tales stood out on his long arms. "Still think you're crazy," he said. "But probably doing the right thing."

"Won't know until I try." Patch smiled.

He's DOING THE RIGHT THING."

"Yes," the Shining One said. "But sometimes it doesn't feel that way."

"That's where faith comes in."

"Exactly," the Shining One agreed.

YOU'RE MAKING IT UP." Erin wanted to cover her ears. The story was incredible.

Stan held her hand. "I tried to hold back," he said. "I didn't want to see you hurt."

Erin wondered if the witness was reliable. Something was missing, something that didn't make sense.

"She was there, Erin." Stan pointed to Ferret Girl.

"Why didn't you tell me before, Cindy?" Erin said.

"Wasn't sure I could trust you," the girl said. Her dark hair was as dull as her eyes. "Soon as Stan gave the word, I knew it was okay."

"And you were the only survivor?"

Cindy refused to meet Erin's eye, but that was her way. "I was left for dead. Too small for anyone to bother with. When the dust settled, I ran."

"Have you told Patch?"

"Never! It was his fault. I hate him."

Erin wondered if the girl ever blinked.

"When the bombs exploded, he ran as fast as he could. He was pushing and shoving, screaming, 'Let me out!' "

"He didn't try to help?"

"You kidding?" Cindy put a hand on one hip. "He ran past Amber . . . his girlfriend. She was crawling, bloody. Patch couldn't get by quick enough."

Stan gave Erin an *I tried to warn you* look.

She didn't know where to turn. Patch was guilty. It was clear. She finally saw the truth.

I'M SURE HE THOUGHT HE WAS DOING THE RIGHT THING in telling you," Patch said. "So did that girl. What's her name?"

"Cindy."

Nothing was making sense to Erin. "So you don't deny killing them?"

"I'm glad Cindy got out. I don't remember her, but I wasn't close to everyone. There were hundreds."

"Patch, you've got to tell me the truth."

"That isn't what happened, okay? But there's no need to give you the details when you've made up your mind. You once said you wanted to believe me. Don't you still?" Erin said nothing. "Because if you don't, it doesn't really matter what I say."

ERIN MAILED THE LETTER but the moment she dropped it in the box, she felt guilty. As though she'd betrayed Patch. She was the cause of the conflict between Stan and Patch. It was her fault.

I'm done.

She asked her parents to come and get her. She didn't trust anyone anymore. Since all the phone lines were monitored a letter would work fine. She didn't know if she was ready to talk to her mom yet, anyway.

GASPS FLEW UP LIKE SPARKS. Why was this happening? Patch knew that somehow he was at the center of the trouble.

Stan and his crew had massed near the stage, arms crossed, a wall of protection for the speaker. Patch saw Tiffany shrug, her friends staring with identical O-shaped mouths. The Tattooed Rats were surrounded, outnumbered. Angry eyes tore into them.

Gary raised a strong arm. His group quieted. "Friends," he said, "we forgive you." A sea of marked men and women, moved toward the exit. Some were crying.

Stan led a cheer. The man up front tried to calm the crowd.

Patch followed his friends out, looking back to see Erin slip closer to Stan.

65

NANCY HAD USED HER GLASS CUTTER to carve out small mirrored ovals. The blank dots were glued over the faces of Mary, John the Baptist, Paul the apostle, Jesus, and others clipped from her hidden Bibles. They spun when Nancy tweaked the mobile.

As the blank faces slowed, Nancy stared. Her own face was reflected in miniature within each drop.

"Lots of work," she said to herself. "Got an A-plus, though." Great art project if you don't mind being accused of being a traitor.

Nancy's creatures had returned. Worse than ever. They bounced from bed to dresser and splashed in the sink. A few flung burning missiles her way. They struck beneath her skin, tearing, searing. Some slid to her side, whispering loud enough for only her to hear.

MOLLY THOUGHT IT WAS WORTH ONE MORE TRY. Anything to get that journal back. She had poured out her life and soul into that book. It made her furious to think of that thing pawing through her private thoughts.

That night Molly crept to Trevor's house. She hoped that the two monsters would be gone, that the door would be wide open, and that she'd see her precious journal resting on the kitchen counter. *Not likely,* she thought. But she had to do something.

Even if they were there, she'd ring the doorbell and calmly ask for what was hers. She would threaten to tell the WPA about their presence, turn them in unless she got what she wanted.

Of course, nothing went as planned. Molly lost her nerve when Trevor opened the door. He was calm, smiling, hair neatly combed. In disguise. Seeing him in the flesh terrified her.

"You're not human!"

She ran. She was alone, her legs churning. Then she heard heavy steps following behind. Trevor and his "father" must be following. Thankfully, she was almost home.

"It's not logical," she said to herself. "Not possible. Ridiculous." She panted, slowing. Another block and she'd be safe.

Her pulse peaked and then began to relax. She took another long look back. Something tripped her, a leathery tail thick as a telephone pole.

Trevor stood before her, teeth bared.

66

D<small>R. M</small>AX <small>MADE IT OFFICIAL.</small> Nancy was healed and ready to leave.

Fit in at all costs. That's what her parents did and Nancy realized the soundness of that advice. "Differences destroy." How often had she heard that mantra?

Nancy had been diagnosed with an "unsafe obsession with religious artifacts and imagery." The treatment had been tedious, mostly talking and talking, and talking. The Bible was myth, legend, fairy tale. That's what they'd told her over and over.

Why, then, she wondered, was it such a threat?

She had to give in or stay in this horrible place. A short but violent scene ultimately brought freedom. It had happened only hours before.

Nancy had been sitting across from Dr. Max, unable to focus on his monotonous brainwashing, when demons began pulling at his hair, tugging on his glasses. He seemed oblivious even when they screamed into his stethoscope.

"You must face the truth," Dr. Max said. Nancy pretended to listen. "Time spent on spiritual pursuits drains your time and energy for more valuable efforts toward peace and tolerance." Nancy nodded. "Accept responsibility for your actions," he continued, "or lose your place in society and learn to survive *alone*."

Nancy knew her parents were watching from behind the two-way mirror, looking for signs of improvement, some show of strength.

She knew what she had to do.

"Evil must be destroyed," Nancy said, conviction in her voice. She attacked the mobile, clawing until she yanked it down. The mirrors shattered when they hit the tile. Nancy stomped each picture. "I renounce your lies!"

"Good," the doctor said. Nancy imagined her parents clapping.

"Tolerance is truth," Nancy intoned. "Friends are family. Differences destroy."

Not long later, success. She was free.

67

MOLLY SPRANG FROM HER MATTRESS, SWEATING. The last thing she remembered was a towering reptile staring her in the eye. The flicking tongue, the father-and-son monsters, that tail blocking her path, tripping her.

She'd felt claws at her neck, poking, squeezing. Then, "Stop! We'll use her later," a raspy voice said and the two turned away. Her head thumped to the concrete.

Had it been real? Or a nightmare?

Molly heard a knock. It was her mother, and she looked worried. "Claudia brought you home. She found you curled up on the sidewalk. Were you sick?"

Molly rubbed the bump on the back of her head. "Maybe. I don't remember . . ."

Her mother tucked Molly in. "You're lucky to have such a friend."

THEY DROVE UP A STEEP INCLINE and familiar houses whipped past. Then Nancy saw the big maple across the street from her house.

She was home.

Granger stood at her doorway. He rushed to help her with her suitcase. "Your mom told me you were coming home today. You okay?"

"Fine," she said. She couldn't tell him she expected something to jump out at her from behind every bush. Her eyes made it clear.

"You still see them, don't you?" he said.

MOLLY SHOWERED, then brushed her hair in front of her white vanity. She pulled it into a ponytail.

Did mirrors speak the truth? This one said she looked perfect . . . at least from the outside.

She reached beneath her mattress and pulled out her thin spiral notepad. She had a couple of minutes before breakfast. She wrote:

> *Why do I hate myself, God?*
> *Why don't I fit in?*
> *Are you really there?*

She added a second question mark.

Patch could help, she thought. *Maybe he could even explain these creatures I think I see.*

Molly called Claudia. "I need his e-mail," she said.

OF COURSE, MOLLY," Claudia said, waving as she spoke on the phone. "Here it is. Please tell him 'hey' for me."

"Good work," Trevor said. "Done with her journal yet?"

"I'm just getting to the good parts." Claudia smiled. *What a handsome guy.*

68

BELIEVE IN FORGIVENESS, PATCH," Stan said, hands out, imploring. "Second chances. Erin assures me you have changed."

They talked outside the coffee shop on neutral ground.

"I'm not sure I'm ready to come back," Patch said. He felt like running. Why should he give Stan the benefit of the doubt? "What about the Tattooed Rats?" He wasn't about to forget his friends.

"Look, forget about them. They're not worth the trouble," Stan said. "Aren't you tired of being seen as one huge mistake?"

How could Stan always know what he was thinking?

"I'm sure you didn't mean to poison our fruit supply." He put his long arm around Patch. "Sometimes it's just best to admit your mistakes and move on."

Patch pulled away. "How can I help?" Hadn't he promised God that he wouldn't say a harsh word to, let alone think a bad thought about, this guy? This was another test. "Yeah, okay, Stan. I'll be there."

DON'T DO IT," the shorter angel said aloud. The teen couldn't hear him. "Please think, Patch." The assistant and the Shining One watched the scene.

"He's trying to follow God's will." The tall angel stretched his wings as if he were about to go hang gliding.

"But he could get hurt."

"Or he could grow," the Shining One said.

Y̶OUR FAVORITE." Stan swept the steaming mocha coffee toward Erin with a flourish.

"Charming," Erin said flatly. "Why?"

"I've been feeling bad about being so harsh with your friend. You like him, so he must have some good qualities."

"You don't have the whole picture . . ." she began. How could she explain?

"Guilty," Stan said, hands aloft. "That's why I've invited him to a Tract Drop. Don't give me that look. It's nothing dangerous. A group of us goes out after midnight and sets out as many gospel flyers as we can."

"I can't believe he agreed."

"Seemed excited about it. He's going to have a good time. Maybe make some friends."

"Thanks, Stan." She sipped her drink, then took his hand.

T̶HINK I MADE THE RIGHT CALL, Gary?" Patch asked.

"No. But I see what you're doing. And why. Especially since we were banished. Maybe you can build a bridge. Personally, I wouldn't trust Stan to return a library book for me, but if you've prayed . . ."

"I have. And I know you'll pray for me."

"Then pass out those tracts. Maybe someone will find the Truth."

Patch nodded. *That's what this was all about.*

The old stomach pains had been coming back more often. Conflict was the cause. He felt like a general fighting on too many fronts, battling Stan, his odd landlord, Erin.

He vowed to keep his suffering silent. No one else had to know. Who would care anyway?

E̶RIN WISHED SHE'D NEVER SENT HER PARENTS the letter. Now they would have details about her location.

I had to tell them. How else would they have believed the note was from me? They had to see my own handwriting.

But now things were starting to work out. Stan and Patch were getting along. Maybe miracles do happen. She should have waited, trusted a little.

But why wouldn't Patch tell her the whole truth? What was he hiding? If that's what Christians did, she didn't want any part of the game.

Time to go home. She imagined the bear hug Terry would have for her.

69

"Hот off the press. Get 'em here." Stan the Man stood on a raised platform near the noisy printing machines, looking like a too-tall and too-old newspaper boy. Patch smiled. He couldn't help it. Everything worked for Stan. He made life look easy.

Stan looked Patch right in the eye and put out a hand. "You made it, man. Thanks for coming. Having you here will be a huge help. You're setting a good example for those Rats of yours."

"Appreciate you putting in a good word with the elders."

"How else could you have taken part?" Stan smiled. "Happy to help."

Patch felt special, sort of. *Watch it*, he thought. Why the warning bells, the sour stomach? Others seemed impressed that he was in with Stan the Man. That made Patch feel good, almost accepted. Kind of cool.

Stan tossed him a pack of 250 flyers tied with twine. "See you later." And he was already on to the next volunteer. That was it? Patch wondered.

"Aren't you going too?" Patch asked.

Stan looked down at him from the platform. "You kidding? Personal stuff, you know." No, Patch didn't know. Unless Stan was referring to Erin. That had to be it. He was trying to make him jealous. It wasn't going to work.

As Patch moved away, other volunteers paired off or went as threesomes. But no one said a word to him. He was on his own.

70

I KNEW ABOUT AMBER," ERIN SAID. "He told me everything."

"Not quite. You didn't know Patch betrayed her." Stan said.

"He made a horrible mistake."

Stan nodded. "But he cared for that girl. Why would he leave a friend to die alone? I couldn't, could you?"

"Maybe that's not what happened."

"That's exactly what happened! The alarm was tripped by an animal hitting a sensor wire. Cindy said so."

Erin was stunned. "Patch never said . . ."

"Why would he? People started leaving. Unfortunately a team of WPA enforcers were there. A spy turned them all in."

"You don't mean?"

"Exactly. Patch got his reward and his family and friends were scattered to the wind. Including Amber. Some were killed, most imprisoned."

"But I thought they all died. Except for Cindy. That's what she said."

"She exaggerates." Stan shook his head. "Doesn't matter. What matters is that Patch didn't tell you the whole story. He tried to scam you into feeling sorry for him."

Erin remembered all those times he'd woken up screaming, claiming nightmares. All an act? She couldn't believe it. Why had Patch lied to her? She couldn't wait to get out of this place and away from these people. *I know*, she thought. *I won't have anything to do with him. Not another word*, she vowed.

Then she had another thought.

What if her letter was chosen by the government for random screening? Besides taking forever, she might have given away the Christian underground.

She'd have to e-mail someone. That way she could get out quicker. Claudia.

All Erin had to do was find a computer.

NOTHING TO DO BUT FOLLOW THROUGH.

Patch headed downtown. The skyscrapers and twenty-four-hour luxury shopping malls lit the sky like Las Vegas at night. Stan told him to leave the booklets on every windowsill. "No one will bother you" had been the promise. But could he trust a syllable from Stan's mouth?

It was lonely work, but maybe someone would find out about Jesus. That would make it worth the trouble. And maybe he could help build a bridge and open the doors for the Tattooed Rats. They needed someone who would listen.

Patch didn't like to believe it, but he knew it was true: God could use even a guy like Stan.

HEY, ERIN," Patch said as he approached. "Went well. Unloaded all the leaflets."

He expected maybe a grin, an "atta-boy," something. But she wouldn't meet his eye. He tried to get in her face. Joke a little. "What's-a-matter?

Stan got your tongue?" She refused to smile. "What's wrong?"

Then it hit him. "What have they been saying now?"

"Nothing, Patch. You're not the center of every conversation, you know. Much as you might want to be."

Patch turned and headed home, exhausted. It had all been for nothing.

C AN'T BELIEVE IT, TREVOR," Claudia said, looking up from Molly's journal. "Patch is an old friend of yours?" She wanted to get to know this guy better. Had a good feeling about him.

"Of me and my father," Trevor said.

"Bet you can hardly wait to find him." Claudia underlined another passage.

Trevor nodded. "You have no idea."

W HY WOULD I MAKE UP A STORY like that?" Molly eyes were puffy and felt red. She daubed at them with a tissue, rubbed the bump on her scalp.

Her mother walked back and forth, arms crossed. "What will your father say? Tell you what. Let's pretend we never talked."

Molly nodded and headed toward the door for school.

"Trevor seemed like such a sweet boy," her mother called after her.

THE MAN IN THE VAN WAS IMPATIENT. As soon as Granger took Nancy's luggage, he sped off.

"What's wrong, Nancy?" Granger said as he walked her up the driveway.

Nancy was on the verge of tears. "Nothing. I'm fine."

Nancy's mom hurried from the front step to her daughter. "You'll have to leave, son," she said.

"Could I talk to her for a minute?" Granger heaved her suitcases.

"I don't think she's ready for that."

Nancy seemed to melt into her mother. She would have fallen if Granger hadn't taken her hand.

"Guess you're right." He said his good-byes. "I'll check back later. There's something I have to talk to you about, Nancy." Her face was pale, sickly. "But only when you're feeling better."

ANOTHER ONE? But, I don't—" Cheryl McCry slammed down the phone. "The director always chooses me for the juvenile offenders. He knows I hate kids."

She shot out an e-mail to her team. "If I've got to suffer, so do they." Then, her day ruined, she flipped open a file.

What? "Missing?" she said aloud. "Again?" Heads turned, popping up over low cubicle walls.

Bad habit, talking to myself. She clamped her lips and stared at the picture of Patrick Johnson: missing. *What's going on with those two undercover agents—they're supposed to be tracking him! Guess I'll have to visit the school, find out what's going on.*

72

THEY MAKE ME SICK," said a girl wearing green lipstick.

"Why?" Marty said. "They're incredible. Where else can a guy get a good dose of violence these days?" In robotic tone he continued: "These presentations keep me on the path of peace."

Cheryl McCry stomped into the room, pushed a few buttons, and the wall-sized video monitor clicked on to blue. Power on. Videos showed long shots of bombs dropping and flares spinning in arcs across the sky.

"The point of impact," she began, "was here." Her laser slowed to a circle around a scene of smoke and fire. People running, bodies strewn. Close-ups and more close-ups.

Two girls in the back had heads on their desks. "Look here!" Ms. McCry bellowed. "The law requires that you watch." The ashen-faced teens looked up, hands on their stomachs.

"Only by viewing such scenes will you understand the damage caused by those who reject the status quo." Ms. McCry pointed to several groups running. The camera work was unsteady. Another close-up. The terror of a mother and her small child a moment before the explosion.

"Once upon a time," Ms. McCry said, "we used to show kids bloody car accidents to get them to drive safely. This is a new era. Now we show this carnage to remind you of the folly of spiritual pursuits." Several more students looked shaken. Success.

"Questions?" she said, her lower lip jutted as though daring anyone to raise a hand.

Marty said. "What was going on in that last scene? Oh yeah, and can we see the gross parts again?" He pounded a buddy next to him.

"We were assisting the injured, of course."

"Someone survived?" Marty said, overplaying a double take. "Don't see how."

"All you've seen so far were warning shots."

"Ma'am," Molly said, hand up. "Could you tell us where this was, please?"

"Certainly." Ms. McCry told how her team rooted out a nest of underground radicals. "We gave them the chance to turn themselves in," she said. "But they chose to fight."

Patch had told Molly that he and his friends were never given a chance to surrender. "They blasted us out," he had said. He said he watched the whole thing.

From what she could see, Patch had been telling the truth. And now they used this footage as propaganda to keep kids in line?

"But I understood no one survived," Molly said.

Ms. McCry looked as though she'd been slapped. "Who told you that?"

73

Granger was gone and Nancy was glad.

Feeling cold, she hugged herself as she walked into the house. Her mother fussed over a teapot. Nancy longed in vain for a hopeful word, a hug.

Instead she made the first move. "You don't have to worry," Nancy said. "I've learned my lesson. I understand how important it is to maintain order in our homes, workplaces, schools, and government." She continued as her mother stared.

"Grades are all that matter. I want to make good grades in school and make you and Dad proud. Just fit in." Her mother nodded. Nancy poured herself a tall glass of orange juice. "Mom, can I ask you a question?"

Her mother turned to face her but was silent. Nancy knew that meant, *Go ahead if you must.* She looked like she was about to have a tooth drilled.

"Sometimes I think that there are . . ." How could she put this? Maybe she shouldn't say another word.

Her mom sat at the kitchen table sipping her tea. Nancy looked out the sliding-glass door to the pool, emptied already in case of an early frost. Dad was always so cautious.

"Mom, do you see that?" She pointed to a demon stumbling near the end of the board. Unsteady, swaying.

Her mother stood and stared, making small choking sounds as the creature leaped, spun high in the air, grabbed his scaly legs tight to his chest, and fell. Nancy waited for the crash, but the thing bounced like a rubber ball. Up and down, higher and higher, laughing. She covered her ears at the piercing chortle.

Her mother's cup and saucer shattered on the tile, tea spreading. "You brought them home with you."

"So I'm not the only one," Nancy said.

74

WHAT'D YOU TELL HER, CINDY?" Patch followed close, reaching for her.

She spun. "Keep your hands away from me." Her narrow nose was greasy from sweat.

"I barely touched you."

Stan and his crew arrived, circling Patch, almost as if they'd been following him.

"You okay, Cin?"

"He's bothering me." She stepped toward Stan. "He grabbed my arm."

What?

"Why are you hurting this girl?" Stan poked a finger into Patch's face. The others pushed in.

Patch wished he could have gotten a minute alone with Cindy before the gang arrived. What had she told Erin? The mess kept getting more tangled.

He wracked his memory, flipping through scattered images. No matter how hard he tried, he couldn't recall Cindy's face. And it wasn't one he should easily forget.

Of course, he hadn't known everyone.

But if she knew Amber, as she claimed, his path should have crossed hers. He had to find out for sure.

*T*ONIGHT, JUST PAST MIDNIGHT, and you're all invited," Stan said. He sat at a table, long legs perched on a chair, enjoying a drink at the coffee shop. Heads nodded. He liked the attention. "I'm sure many souls were saved because of the last Tract Drop. This time it's going to be even bigger, the best one yet. I really would like to see us work together." Stan looked toward the ceiling. "Think what that would mean to the elders."

"We *should* all try to get along," Tiffany said in agreement. Some of the other kids in the coffee shop rolled their eyes. Erin felt like it.

But others agreed with, "Wow," "Deep," and "Profound."

"Maybe we *should* help with the tract distribution, make it a party," Tiffany said, twisting a thick spiral of hair in her finger. "Heard everyone had fun last time. And you never know who you might meet! I think it's what God would want us to do. You know," she said, "there are many ways of looking at him."

"Or her," a girl piped up. Tiffany giggled.

"We'll be there," she said.

At that moment Erin charged in, headed straight for Stan. "This is the only time I'll ask you. What happened to Patch? I saw him. His face is bruised, cut. He wouldn't say a word."

"He didn't tell you, and you think he's going to open up to me?"

75

Ms. McCry's eyes flashed. "Patrick Johnson. Went by 'Patch.' Know where he is?"

Molly wished she did.

"He's a liar," McCry said. "And a murderer. He put hundreds more at risk, including my WPA officers, who give their all to keep you safe."

"So you're blaming a kid?" Molly whistled low. "Must be some kind of Superteen to outsmart a woman like you."

The door at the back of the room opened. Had McCry called in the troops already?

The woman's face was red as a fire hydrant. She jammed her fists into her pockets. "That boy could have saved them all by just telling me their numbers and their location." She seemed to be trying to calm herself. "He refused."

"And actions have consequences," a new voice said. "Even if we don't always appreciate the results." It was Nancy. She took an empty seat.

"So this guy, Patch," Molly said, "our fellow student, bombed his friends? C'mon, you can't come up with a better story than that?" She was over the line and tired. Visions of demons can wear a girl down. Molly felt like surrendering, taking it all back.

McCry was standing now. "That young man brought the horror on himself."

Molly remembered the stories Patch had told her, of pounding on the door to the cavern, his cries of warning, being forced to watch.

"Patch didn't actually kill anyone, did he?" Molly said. "You get full credit."

Ms. Strong sputtered and McCry yanked a remote device from her belt and stabbed a string of numbers. As if someone had cut a hole in a bag of sand, men and women streamed through the doors.

Two grabbed Molly and pulled her away. McCry followed.

AFTER McCRY LEFT, THE UPROAR FADED.

"Poor Molly," Claudia said, breaking the quiet. "Guess she missed New Peace." Laughter rippled.

Marty slumped in his seat. "Is she stupid, or what?"

"You got that right," Nancy said. "Ms. Strong, may I address my classmates?" Ms. Strong nodded, and Nancy stood. "Forgiveness is the hallmark of our culture. We all make mistakes, but must forget the past and move on."

Nancy walked up one aisle and down the next. "Social order matters more than life itself. Without it, our lives would collapse." She squeezed Marty's shoulder. "I've learned my lesson. To question authority is to question truth. We have no right. The WPA has our best interests at heart. And this tottering little planet would do much better if we all realized it."

"She okay, Marty?" Claudia whispered.

"Normal as ever," he said.

MS. STRONG COULDN'T SPEAK, couldn't move. A green claw, long-nailed and large, reached from behind and grabbed a hunk of her hair. She bellowed like a bull and fell. "Let go!"

T REVOR AND HIS PARTNER, an older man in a loose sweater, faced Cheryl McCry. Trevor scuffed one shoe on the other like a kid caught with the cookies and the jar. "We're close. Confessions should be forthcoming. In fact, we think—"

"Whining annoys me," Ms. McCry said. "And that's the same line you gave me last time." She grabbed a chunk of shoulder from the man and boy. Her fingernails indented their skin. "This is a public relations nightmare. How can one kid elude the WPA?"

"We'll get him," Trevor said.

"You have no alternative," Ms. McCry said. "And if you two relocate again without approval, I'll have you imprisoned." She slammed the door on her way out.

The man massaged his shoulder. "She doesn't have a clue." He yawned wider, wider still, until his mask cracked and slid off. The beast beneath stretched upward. Skin curled back like an old snake hide. The boy followed his mentor's example.

"Why are we waiting?" Trevor asked.

"Because those are our orders."

"Hard to breathe in those things. I don't see why we have to hide."

"You will someday," the more experienced demon said. "Subtlety is our greatest weapon. He stomped to the fridge. "You eat that leftover pizza?" His tail scraped gouges into the tile.

WHY DID YOU TELL THAT STORY, CINDY?" They were walking together. "Please stay. Please answer me." If only he could get her to admit she was lying. Then everything would straighten itself out.

Cindy kicked a rusting can. "I don't hate you, Patch. I really don't." She pulled her elbows in tight as though expecting someone to hit her. "I just didn't, um, remember, that's all." She looked nervous. "I gotta go. Stan wouldn't want me talking to you."

"If you honestly don't remember, can you at least tell Erin that?"

"No." Cindy backed away. "Why do you care what she thinks?"

"She's my friend. I want her to know the truth."

"I have friends, too, and I care what they think," she said. "That's why I do what they say."

"I tried to save Amber. I tried to lead the attackers away from the hiding place."

"That's not what I heard. But if you really want to prove yourself, maybe you could come to the big Tract Drop tonight."

Patch wondered whether or not he should take the bait. But he could tell from her face that she was sincere, so he listened to all the details.

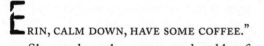

77

"E RIN, CALM DOWN, HAVE SOME COFFEE."

She strode to the counter, ordered her favorite. She forced herself to breath, to relax. "So you didn't have anything to do with it?" she asked as she sat down next to Stan.

"I don't hate him," Stan said. He lowered his voice. "I feel sorry for him."

"But how could you let Cindy repeat things if you knew they weren't true?" She decided to challenge Stan face to face. Either Patch or Stan had to be lying.

"I thought they were. Still do. Besides it's Cindy's word against his."

"But Patch was there."

"So was Cindy," Stan said, smiling. "It's confusing, I know. And it'll only get worse. That's why you've got to cut ties with him."

"But I want the truth," Erin said. In fact, she wanted the truth even more than she wanted out. Longed for an end to the endless discussions, the hard decisions. When she got home she'd let her mom pick out her meals, her clothes, even tell her when to go to bed. No more thinking.

"If you aren't part of our group," Stan said, "you can't be a true Christian." He tapped his watch. "You never know how much time you have."

"But Patch said—"

"Forget what he told you! How can you trust someone who's hurt so many people?"

That made sense, Erin thought. And that was saying a lot these days.

PATCH HAD BEEN WAITING OUTSIDE. He followed Erin as she left the coffee shop. "I've got to talk to you."

"No, you don't." She took longer strides. "Tonight's my last worship service." Patch stopped. "And you're not invited," she said over her shoulder. "I'm leaving as soon as my parents get here."

"They know where to find you?" Patch said. He looked suddenly scared.

"I told them to pick me up at the old fountain. Town center. I wanted a public spot."

"When?" Patch questioned.

"Tonight, just after midnight."

"You don't know what you've done," Patch said. He thought of Cindy's invitation.

Erin shrugged. "Sure I do," she said. "I found a way to escape."

He couldn't explain to her, didn't have time. Patch turned and ran.

W HY, MOLLY? WHY?" Her mother's eyes dripped. "You've shamed us again."

"I can't stand lies. Especially official ones." Molly crossed and uncrossed her legs in Principal O'Connor's office.

"They're a part of life, Molly! They keep people from tearing each other apart." Her father nodded, in on the secret.

"So all I have to do is apologize?" Molly asked the principal.

"Forgotten," Mr. O said. "You're a success story, Molly. This minor relapse can be overlooked."

"You don't want to miss the prom, do you?" her mother said. "How many boys have asked you?"

"I've lost count," Molly said. "So this whole mess disappears with one little lie?" Molly held a hand over her mouth. "Excuse me, I don't feel well."

Alone in the bathroom she took stock. *Another second chance. What more could I ask for?*

Ms. Strong struggled to get up. Another yank toppled her and the class saw her take what looked like a stomp to the stomach. She squirmed.

A familiar anxiety surged through Nancy. She wanted to look away but couldn't.

"Who did that?" Ms. Strong screamed. "Which of you?" She pointed at Marty, Nancy, and the others.

Nancy watched the thing stroll through the wall, claws full of Ms. Strong's short, silver hair. His stench remained.

In the hall, Granger caught up with Nancy and helped carry library books. She had jumped back into studying, extra homework every night.

"Heard about the fireworks in Ms. Strong's class." "Can't talk now," she said, her mouth a grim line.

It was now or never. Granger took the chance.

"Do you know what demons are?" he said.

79

THE SHINING ONE AND HIS ASSISTANT saw Patch tear past.

"They're coming," the young angel said.

His teacher looked more serious. "The forces are gathering."

PATCH DIDN'T STOP RUNNING until his breath came in gasps. He would have kept going, fallen from the pain, but he had to think about the others. They would die, or at the least be taken prisoner. Erin didn't know or she wouldn't have brought the WPA to their doorstep.

They were all to meet at the fountain center at midnight for a Tract Drop. It made sense—after the success of the last event, Stan wanted to score another success. But the whole group would be right in the middle of their work when Erin's parents came.

Patch had to say something, try to stop this mess.

Because he was certain Erin's parents wouldn't be alone.

Patch's reaction was weird, Erin thought. What was the big deal? She was one person. If she left, it wouldn't matter. She had to admit, though, it kind of made her feel good to see Patch so concerned, though she doubted it was over her.

"Erin to God," she said aloud. "I'm not sure what's happening, but please protect Patch. My friend." That was it. She couldn't think of anything else to say.

She waited. Nothing happened. No wave of peace flowed through her. Not like when she'd gotten together with Nancy and Patch and prayed for Granger.

That time she knew God was listening. He had answered.

This time it felt like she was talking only to herself. She saw a homeless man in a cardboard shelter. He looked up at her, hand out.

"God bless you." Several teeth were missing.

Too bad he hasn't done much for you. Erin stepped around the man.

Patch looked for an ally among the adults, pleading his case with the man who'd had a stroke, a heavyset woman with tiny dolllike features, and the leader of the elders. They were all standing, serious.

"Erin didn't know. But I bet her family will call the WPA," Patch began. "Stan and the others will be walking into a trap."

"I don't believe you." Doll Lady smiled. "I like Stan," she said. "And I think you're simply trying to make him look foolish."

"No. That's not it. I want people to learn about Jesus." Patch knew he wasn't connecting.

"Then why are you throwing a wrench into Stan's careful plans? Sounds like you're on Satan's side."

Patch wasn't getting through. He had only one more chance. "The guy has lied about me repeatedly. To Erin and the others. He hates me." He didn't want to, but the truth had to come out. Maybe, finally, someone would start listening to him.

"Perhaps with good reason," the woman said. "You know you're not welcome here. You and the rest of those Tattooed Rats. A pack of liars."

"But I'm trying to warn you. Trying to protect everybody." He sensed a pounding headache coming on.

"Pretending to be the hero," the woman said with a pasted-on smile. She looked at the others. "How do you know about this so-called attack unless you helped plan it? I suspect that you want to ruin our efforts to tell people about Christ, and Stan's reputation in the process."

"Maybe," said the man who'd had the stroke, "he's trying to help." The others shook their heads.

The bearded man sighed. Patch could see he'd had enough. "From what I hear," he said slowly, "you're the one with the problem telling the truth."

This wasn't working. They think I'm setting them up. He'd have to do something on his own.

"Good riddance," Doll Lady said as Patch left.

80

Nancy squirmed. "Look, Granger, I have to run."

"Demon got your tongue?"

"Not funny."

"Neither is thinking I'm crazy." He slogged down the hall. "Guess I'm the only one who sees them."

"You're not," she whispered.

He'd heard her. He turned, a question in his eyes.

No pressure, Molly," Principal O'Connor said. "Take the night to think it over."

When she got home she understood. On the dining room table lay an offering fit for a princess. Chocolates, makeup, hair extensions, ribbons, bows. Books, music.

"Just say you're sorry, honey," her dad said. "And everything here is yours."

All she had to do was blame stress, sickness, or worry. Anything but the truth. "So it's okay to question God but not your teacher." Molly said.

Her parents smiled and shrugged and nodded.

"That doesn't make sense. Questions are taboo unless you already know the answers?" She could see in their faces that she needed to back off. To play the game she needed access to the players. She'd lose that in a mental hospital.

Molly's smile was drenched with sweetness. "I'm sorry, Mom. I was wrong." She gave her a long, strong hug. "I don't know what I was thinking." Molly surprised herself at how easily the lies poured out. Her father came close. Group hug.

HERE'S A VID CLIP I snatched from the Web," Marty said. "It's the town fountain. Water spurts 150 feet into the air every fifteen minutes. Light show too. Look here." The others gathered.

"Midnight tonight, then?" Claudia said. She offered to drive.

"Looking forward to it," Trevor said.

"You going to warn them?" she said jokingly.

"Are you kidding? I like to keep my prey—I mean my friends—off guard." Trevor's jaw clicked as he grinned.

YOU'RE SURE WE'RE DOING THE RIGHT THING?" her husband asked.

"Positive." Erin's mom handed Erin's letter to Ms. McCry. "I thought you'd want it for evidence."

"This should end your daughter's troubles," Ms. McCry said. She scanned the details. She was well acquainted with the fountain.

"What about the boy?" Erin's father said.

"We'll make an example of him," Ms. McCry said.

"By the way, we're not interested in having him placed here again," Mrs. Morgan said. The women laughed, and little Terry looked up. His mother took him in her arms.

81

THE SHINING ONE STOOD BY, wishing he could do something besides wait. His companion put words to their thoughts. "You sure we can't help?"

"Not yet. But soon."

They watched as Patch took another kick to the stomach, then a row of knuckles in the back of his neck. The attackers kept coming, taking turns.

ANOTHER MINUTE and he'd fall. But he had to keep trying.

"Stan! Erin told me herself! Her parents will be there tonight!"

"Blaming her makes it even worse. You're a coward."

"Don't you see?" Patch cried out. "They'll be waiting. I'm trying to keep you from making a huge mistake."

"You mean getting all the credit." Stan circled him. "You're delusional. First, Erin loves it here and second, she would never ever rat on her friends. Like you would. If she'd written a letter like you claim, she would have told me. We're very close." Stan shoved Patch and he fell.

"Tonight's drop goes as planned. People out there need to know the Truth, and your stories aren't going to stop us. You've been disinvited."

Patch was on his hands and knees, head hanging.

"You have two jobs, Patch. Staying away from me and making sure nothing strange happens tonight."

Patch's ulcer bore into his stomach wall. He curled into a ball.

I'LL BE LOOKING FOR YOU," Trevor said, hanging up.

"Who was that?" Claudia asked driving heavy footed. Marty was in the backseat.

"Old friend. Wants to see the fountain too."

Claudia floored it. "Let's be the first ones there."

PATCH LAY THERE PRAYING and felt peace seep through him. Strength returned; his tired, beaten body was warm. He could move his limbs again, though his head still ached. He couldn't see the two angels standing at his side, silently urging him on.

I know what the Beast wants.

He was ready for McCry.

It was the only way.

THROUGH THE CROWDED COURTYARD, Stan, Tiffany, and the others walked side by side passing out chocolate candy. The courtyard was packed, streetlights making the night bright. People were smiling, talking. It was like a carnival—bright lights, live music.

Each candy wrapper included a Scripture verse. Others passed out brochures explaining who God was and why everyone needed Jesus as their Savior.

Gary watched from the sidelines. He and his friends had been forbidden to take part.

"They can't keep us from praying," he said, tattoos peeking out around his neck and wrist. Amid cheers, the group knelt.

The Shining One, his companion, and dozens of others stood watching, praying. Ready for the attack.

ISN'T IT WONDERFUL?" Doll Lady said as she stood with the other elders. "And to think that young man wanted to stop this effort. What a waste that would have been."

Stan swung by and pretended to offer the woman a brochure. The two clowned. Her face had a glow. "He's such a nice young man," she said, as he continued on.

"People are listening," the bearded elder said. "Souls will be saved."

"Truly an answer to prayer," Doll Lady gurgled.

Alone in her room Molly listened to the music of the hot, skinny star of the hour.

The moody voice made Molly sway, made her wish she could sing too. Nice Principal O'Connor had said she could come late to school today, because of what she'd gone through. She didn't mind being coddled. He was only being kind because she'd done what he wanted. Funny how that worked.

She'd get a charge out of strolling in late to class. No hassles, no fear of being sent to the office. Doing what the rest weren't allowed. That was fun.

Molly took her time combing her hair before the bathroom mirror. She paused to paw through the goodies from her parents. *Everything a girl could need,* she thought. And more. Expensive, new stuff. Things for her hair, her lips, her nails.

It hadn't been so hard. One more lie. She could do it for a living. She had cleared the air with her parents; that was the bottom line. Being an individual, doing and saying her own thing, wasn't worth the trouble.

She heard a knock. "Enter," Molly said. She couldn't decide which beaded headband she wanted to wear. All three were unique.

Her mother came in. "You are beautiful," she said. "My daughter the prom queen." Molly couldn't think of anything modest to say. Instead she hugged her mom. She knew that was what she wanted. "Your father and I are glad you decided to do the right thing."

"Honesty pays," Molly said. The array of gifts covered her dresser, were piled on the ledge behind her sink, overflowed onto a shelf in the bathroom. It hadn't been so tough repeating what they wanted to hear. It was a small price for getting along.

She adjusted the headband again, her hair smooth and shiny. A princess in a jeweled crown. She had it all: looks, brains, and the little things that made life more comfortable.

The mirror doesn't lie. She smiled, teeth gleaming.

GRANGER'S EYES PIERCED HER OWN. "I'm not the only one who sees the creatures?"

Nancy shrugged, wishing she could take it back. No way was she going to admit what had been happening to her. "Claudia heard Molly say she'd seen dragons, demons, creepy-crawlies, whatever." She shifted her weight to her other leg. "Crazy, huh? Who would believe that?"

Granger was about to answer. A bell saved them from the awkward quiet. And Nancy turned to go.

MOLLY HAD NEVER HAD ANYTHING AGAINST SNAKES. No fear. Until now.

She froze, a statue staring. The image writhed before her. Her thick, shiny hair was gone, replaced by spitting, squirming snakes. She couldn't move, couldn't think.

The closer she got to the mirror the more the serpents twisted and struck. She had the sensation of someone pulling on her scalp, yanking hair invisible to her.

She told herself it wasn't real, that she was hallucinating. But she knew better. She could smell that rotted jungle scent.

It was nearly time for class. She grabbed the snakes, pulling as hard as she could. It hurt like crazy and she wanted to cry out, but she didn't want her mom to come running.

Soon the odor wafted away, replaced by a flowery perfume.

"God," she prayed, "please let them be gone."

SITTING IN CLASS WAS A WASTE. Nancy considered telling Granger the truth and wondered what he'd been about to say before the bell rang. Would he laugh? Turn her in? Never speak to her again?

She trusted him, she wasn't sure why. Guess it was because he seemed to care.

Nancy shut her book, put down her pencil, and stared at the clock.

As soon as class was over, she'd find him and get things out in the open.

HER HAIR WAS A MESS, flopped over her eyes, balled up behind her ears.

At least the snakes were gone.

She had to talk to someone. She couldn't keep a secret like this.

In minutes, Molly had separated the twisted strands of her hair, sprayed them wet, and with the blow-dryer and comb managed to look in control again.

Everything was fine. Except for that hissing in her ears. When she took her new earrings out, the slithering noises stopped. All was quiet.

GRANGER?" Molly looked up at him. "What's up?"

"Got to talk you," he said, standing at her door.

"Now?"

His bike was a silver-and-red clump in the grass.

He pursed his lips. "You have a couple minutes?"

Aᴇᴛᴇʀ Eɴɢʟɪsʜ, Nᴀɴᴄʏ ʟᴏᴏᴋᴇᴅ ғᴏʀ Gʀᴀɴɢᴇʀ. He should be coming out of algebra class any second. She had to tell him about the time he'd been in a coma and she and Erin and Patch prayed for him. Together, hands linked.

Never before had Nancy felt so close to understanding that a great and powerful God sat listening for her and heard her.

She had been in the hospital when Granger got out, too dazed to know any of the details. All she knew was that Granger's father was ready to cut off the life-support machines. Then Granger had come back to life. No one used the word *miracle* anymore, but what some would have called a coincidence or good luck Nancy believed could have been an answer to prayer. She knew Patch would say that. But what about Granger?

Only he could tell what had happened to him in that room at New Peace. And maybe, if he said the right things in the right way, she'd be willing to tell him more too.

She might even admit that she too had seen creatures—snarling, darting little things that haunted her at home, around the school, at the pizza place.

The room was empty when she peered in. The math teacher gave her an odd look.

But where was Granger?

83

CLAUDIA WHIPLASHED HER PASSENGERS as she screeched to a stop near the fountain.

Trevor rubbed his neck.

"Nice driving," Marty said.

"Catch you later," Trevor said, and he headed off.

"Good-looking guy," Claudia said, "but weird."

"Too weird even for you?" Mary said, punching her lightly.

They walked toward the fountain as people streamed along the sidewalk.

"What's that?" Claudia said as they passed through two large doors leading into the fountain courtyard. Shops lined the square.

"Looks like an old Halloween costume. The full-body kind."

Claudia picked up the face mask and held it out like a gross bug. She pulled the rubbery ears, opening the blob for a better look. "Trevor!" she screamed. "It's Trevor!"

"CLOSING IN." Ms. McCry was about to snap her phone shut. "I'll call when we have your daughter." She rolled her eyes as she elbowed an officer. "Parents." After a beat she announced, "Set guns to paralyze."

"Aw, boss. Only stun?"

"No whining. Orders from above." The order didn't say anything about her gun, though.

THE SHINING ONE LIFTED HIS WINGS, fluttered them wide. "Any second. Be ready." All angelic eyes turned his way. "Draw your swords." The unsheathing rang like thunder. "Move on my command."

His young charge spread his wings, arm high, sword aloft. "Can't they see us yet?"

"No. But soon." The Shining One was calm. "In God's timing."

THERE HE IS," THE DEMON SAID, pointing at Patch, moving fast on huge, gnarled feet. Others joined him. Ghouls on parade, black and gray nightmares in a line, with Trevor and his mentor among the leaders.

Patch stifled a yell. He stood in the center of the plaza, near the fountain. "So it's in the open, now?"

"We're ready," Trevor said, a towering scaly beast with mouth wide, jaws snapping like a hungry gator.

"Dragon breath," Patch said. "Time to return to your papa, the father of lies. In the name of Jesus, I pray for strength."

His friends, the Tattooed Rats, also pounded on the door of the throne room of heaven. Patch looked to the skies.

"I see them!" he shouted.

TREVOR THE DEMON SENSED TERROR in the other attackers. Hungry with hate, these devils had hoped to swallow souls whole.

His mask gone, Trevor lifted his long, toothy snout to the wind, sniffing. When he saw the Shining One bow his head and close his eyes, Trevor lost all hope.

Other angels stood with swords raised. The face of the Shining One changed from patient to purposed, lines etched dark and deep at his mouth.

"Uh-oh," Trevor moaned. Those winged creeps in white were about to ruin the party.

Trevor heard the order from above: "Cut them down. Scatter them."

The Shining One, majestic and roaring, his sword before him, became a missile intent on its target.

"The weak ones are here," Trevor shouted. He shoved at the other demons, curled into a ball, and rolled down the alley, knocking over garbage cans. "Not my time," he muttered. "Not yet."

The other demons flexed long claws, revealed rows of hidden horns, widened jaws to unleash snapping teeth.

Idiots, Trevor thought. *They'll find out.*

The battle was swift, heated. Demon limbs clattered to the ground, disappearing into acrid smoke. Trevor cowered in the doorway to a smelly mouse hole. His cronies fled or were skewered on the point of the sword. Some shot like hot red rockets toward the heavens, white-winged warriors in pursuit. A few escaped as the angelic forces closed in.

It was clear whose side God was on.

Stupid angels. Trevor hated them.

When he'd seen enough, he transformed into a gnat-sized serpent, winged and irritated enough to sting. He spun his tail, swirled into the darkness.

CHERYL McCRY HEARD SHRIEKS, banging, chilling moans far beyond the muffled cries of the captured. But her eyes said her ears were liars. So strange. Sound but no picture. Must be traffic noise.

No worries. She knew better than to go with her emotions. She valued what she could measure, control with her own hands.

She saw only a few scrambling Christians, running cowards without a thought for those they'd left. And of course, Patch. Her target.

Something was wrong with him. He seemed to be staring, entranced, as though front row at the biggest game of the year. His head bobbed as if watching a tennis match. His expression told her he was seeing things.

Maybe he was crazy.

PATCH SAW THE LAST DEMON obliterated with the flat edge of a broadsword, leaving only a putrid puff of smoke. The Shining One raised a victorious fist and cried, "Hosanna!" in a voice that rocked the entire block.

Patch pumped a fist. "All right!"

McCry marched toward Patch, who stood alone, every eye in the square on him. He uttered not one word.

His time had come.

84

Tiffany, Stan, and the others waited on the fringes, wide eyed. A few tore away, shouting, "Get out! Run!"

The Tattooed Rats advanced, surrounding Ms. McCry and her elite World Peace Alliance officers. Seemingly unafraid, they kept praying.

Patch looked into the woman's face. She looked intent.

"It's time, Mr. Patrick Johnson," Ms. McCry said. "You understand, don't you?"

"You don't scare us." He gestured to the group forming a circle. "No fear anywhere." Gary, Erin, and the rest stood watching.

Ms. McCry gave the signal. A flare raced overhead, lighting the fountain, every face. The arrests began.

Officers dragged underground believers toward the fountain, some fleeing, some weeping. The captured were shackled and appeared stunned. Screams rose.

"Let them go," Patch said.

"I could kill you," she said.

"Why should I listen?"

"Because I could make you a hero."

Believers nearby shouted, "No! Stand firm, Patch! Don't give in!"

"If I switched sides, would you let these people go? I could be your poster child for the success of rehab, for tolerance." He could tell McCry was listening.

The woman looked tired.

"Imagine the headlines," Patch said. "The interviews."

Her eyes narrowed. After a moment's thought, she gave a short, quick nod to an officer. "You've sufficiently scared them," she told her team. "Let them go. All of them."

"Thank you," Patch said.

What have I done?

"I'll assume you're on our side now . . . or you'll regret it," she said, handcuffing him. It was over.

Erin watched the people scatter. They all ran.

She began to sprint away. She felt like smiling, screaming. She was free. They all were.

Except for Patch.

Why would he do this? She stopped and turned back. He had rejected everything he stood for.

McCry's team attacked Patch, drove him to his knees. His face scraped the concrete, streaked red. Erin wanted to go to him but was frozen with fear.

Officers shoved Patch toward a New Peace van.

Erin watched in wonder. *He did this for me. Me. Why?*

She turned and ran again, street after street, lamps lighting her way. Erin wanted to be anywhere but where Patch had turned traitor.

A figure closed in on Erin, a woman in tattered jeans and faded pink T-shirt. She held out a clean white handkerchief and Erin stopped. Talk about out of the blue. She took the gift and wiped her tears. "Thanks. Who are you?"

"A helper." Erin studied the young woman's face, ageless, her hair shining in the shadows. "A friend of Patch's. And yours." The voice was soft but clear.

Erin hesitated, afraid to take the outstretched hand. But she did and felt her soul quake then calm as she soaked up the peace flowing from this person. "What's your name?" Erin said at last.

"Just 'friend.' I'm on your side."

Erin shivered, and the woman was gone without a sound, as if she'd never been there. An angel?

Erin knotted the damp, white handkerchief.

Patch was bruised, bloody, beaten.

McCry pointed to the seat belt. "I'll speak with you in the morning. You're the new poster boy for the World Peace Alliance." Her laugh was shrill. "Gives you chills, doesn't it?" She slammed the sliding door so hard Patch expected it to jump its track.

He put his head in his hands.

"Where to?"

Patch snapped his head up. The driver was his favorite buzzcut barber, tattoos and all.

"I don't understand. You're not supposed to—"

The quiet orderly sat in the front passenger seat. She held a finger to her lips as they drove past WPA troops.

They turned right, the opposite direction from New Peace. "I won't tell if you won't," the barber said, inked biceps bulging. "Might mean my job." He laughed.

Patch had never had a prayer answered quite like this. He had no clue where they were going and didn't care. All he knew was that the Tattooed Rats had risked themselves to help and protect him, and he was proud to be one of them.

He touched the tiny tattoo at his ankle. Even someone like him could be used by God, and he could hardly wait to find out how.